REPEAT

NEAL POLLACK

ALSO BY NEAL POLLACK

FICTION

Jewball
Never Mind the Pollacks: A Rock and Roll Novel
Beneath the Axis of Evil
The Neal Pollack Anthology of American Literature

THE MATT BOLSTER YOGA MYSTERIES

Open Your Heart
Downward-Facing Death

NONFICTION

Stretch
Alternadad

REPEAT

NEAL POLLACK

LAKE UNION

PUBLISHING

Text copyright © 2015 Neal Pollack.

Published by Lake Union Publishing, Seattle.

www.apub.com

Amazon, the Amazon logo, and Lake Union Publishing are trademarks of Amazon.com Inc. or its affiliates.

ISBN-13: 9781477821336
ISBN-10: 1477821333

Cover design by *the*BookDesigners

Library of Congress Control Number: 2014915075

Printed in the United States of America.

For Regina and Elijah, until further notice.

LOS ANGELES

2010

On the morning before his fortieth birthday, Brad Cohen woke up feeling bad. He imagined how this would be written up in the *East Hills Beacon*, the monthly neighborhood circular: "Another loser on the geographical and cultural fringes of Hollywood spent the morning feeling sorry for himself . . ." But then he stopped thinking that. Something wasn't newsworthy when it happened every day. Brad rested on his daily slab of self-pity like a flabby Korean businessman getting soaped down in the basement of a cheap ethnic bathhouse on Wilshire. On this day, though, he felt vindicated in his wallow.

If a man can't feel like a loser at forty, Brad thought, *then when can he?*

Brad opened his eyes, because eventually he had to do that. He was on his back, the best way to sleep according to the book of ayurvedic healing methods that his wife kept on the coffee table. Back sleeping, preferably done with the arms overhead, elbows clasped, opened up the nasal passages, improving airflow. But back sleeping also meant the first thing that Brad saw in the morning was his bedroom ceiling, dotted with little bright yellow stains. How had they gotten there? It looked like someone had flung around a paintbrush dipped in movie-theater popcorn butter. Most likely it was water damage, even though it only rained for about a week here in December and then not at all for the rest of the year. But Brad's landlady hadn't made any repairs to the place since Madonna was like a virgin. Unless the boiler blew up, and even then it was almost impossible to get her to take the ladder out of the shed.

The glow creeping into the room hinted at another day of oppressively cheery Southern California sun. Juliet had hand-cut blackout shades from some dark, denim-style cloth she'd bought on remainder at Michaels. Their frayed edges gathered dust along the floorboards. The shades worked pretty well at dawn, but by 9:00 a.m. most days they were useless. The day's relentlessly sunny demands threatened to drag Brad back from the self-imposed mud pit of his half-remembered career sorrows.

But first he had to run through them one more time.

Brad grew up in Chicago, in the Hyde Park neighborhood. He was the son of an activist and a professor, a combination possible in only about ten zip codes across the country. In those kinds of households, there were always magazines full of ideas and essays written by people with substantial biographies.

Early on, Brad was reading the *Nation*, the *New Republic*, the *New Yorker*, *Harper's*, the *Atlantic*, and several other magazines that were even more boring and had even fewer pictures. Brad didn't really understand most of what he read, though he thought he did. But the *New Century*, the greatest of all American idea magazines, topped the list. Someday Brad would work at the *New Century*. *Someday*, he thought, *I will shape the national conversation.*

It was a reasonable enough ambition for a Jewish pseudointellectual, and Brad was smart enough to make it happen. A solid high school newspaper career combined with internships. An easy acceptance to the University of Chicago, where his father taught, led to a position on a college newspaper. Then he started publishing counterintuitive essays about consumer culture in a start-up smarty-pants called the *Waffler*. One essay, titled "VH1 Stole My Milk Money," actually got excerpted in *Harper's* and *Utne Reader*, and Brad was on his way.

He applied to be a junior editor at the *New Century*, just a summer gig—though not an internship either. They paid $250 a week. This was the rarest of opportunities, and Brad got it, beating out hundreds of other candidates. He moved to DC for the summer, ready to fulfill all his promise.

When he got there, he found that he was no longer the smartest person in the room. In fact, he had no sources and no ideas— which was new to him, because he always had ideas. His entire output at the magazine consisted of a thousand-word piece about fifth-party weirdos running for president and a brief about how the police had railroaded Pee-wee Herman when they'd caught him jerking it in a movie theater. He left a week early, saying he had to get back to Chicago because his dad was ill. That was the end of his career in punditry, the only career he'd ever considered.

The late '90s found him a copywriter at a Chicago ad agency, making nearly $40,000, hardly a tragedy. He had health insurance and a modest pension and a decent amount of free time, which he used to write a novel, find an agent, and actually get the book published with a mainstream house. Called *Going Nuclear*, it was about employees at a Chicago ad agency who try to keep their business running after a terrifying industrial accident wipes out most of the Eastern seaboard. *Going Nuclear* was reviewed, mostly well, in the places where it needed to get reviewed. Janet Maslin, in the *New York Times*, called it a "darkly comic satire of the way we live now." He was interviewed on *Weekend Edition* and profiled in the *Chicago Tribune*. A magazine (which no longer existed) that covered the book industry (which barely still existed) had named him "a writer to watch." They wittily gave him an actual watch, a pretty good one, which Brad still had even though it had stopped running in 2008. Brad had gotten paid reasonably well. He intended to write another book and to proceed with his life, which, despite some early disappointments, had gone about as well as he could have ever hoped.

And then Hollywood, as it likes to do, ruined everything.

One day in the spring of 2000, when the world was innocent and young, the phone rang in Brad's office.

"Hello," he said.

"Is this *the* Brad Cohen?" asked a voice, female, slightly slurry and slightly chirpy.

"It's *a* Brad Cohen."

There followed a streak of laughter that sounded like a mad-woman cackling over a cauldron. If Brad had hung up the phone right there, which he considered, fate would have possibly spared him a decade of debt and humiliation. But instead he waited a bit.

"Oh my God," the voice said. "You're as funny as your book is."

Going Nuclear was certainly wry in places and definitely ironic throughout, but Brad hadn't even laughed out loud while *writing* it, so this wasn't a reaction he'd expected. Later, he learned that no one in Hollywood actually ever read anything, except for trade reviews, spec scripts, and gossipy blog posts. For now, though, Brad still lived in the Midwest, and therefore when he heard praise he thought it was sincere.

"Thank you," he said.

"You're welcome," said the voice.

"Who is this?"

"I'm so sorry," she said. "My name is Alison Shreveport. I'm a literary manager for the Film Strip."

"What's that?"

"It's a company."

"But what does it do?"

"Manages people."

"What kinds of people?"

"Writers, directors. A lot of commercials. Spike Jonze was a client. Before he went into movies."

"OK," Brad said.

He thought she was talking about "Spike Jones," who had written a bunch of novelty songs back in the '40s, including "Der Fuehrer's Face."

"So what do you want with me?" he said.

"I want to manage you, silly," she said.

No one had ever offered to manage Brad before. He could barely even manage himself, so he was tempted by the prospect of having management. It sounded very adult.

One month later he was on a United Airlines flight to LA. He checked into a motel across the street from CBS Television City and drove his rented Honda Civic to an office complex behind a refinery in West LA. The building was all slab concrete and exposed pipes, brightly painted. He got there at 4:00 p.m., right when he was scheduled to, and waited for half an hour, eating M&M's out of a bowl and reading magazine stories about people who were better looking and more successful than him, an experience that would soon become more common for him than going to the bathroom.

Finally, Alison Shreveport appeared. Great tits, great tan, great hair. She wore an all-white jumpsuit and a gold necklace that she couldn't possibly have purchased for herself. She smelled like two glasses of wine.

Brad stood up.

"Is this the great Brad Cohen?" she asked.

"It is," Brad said.

"Hiiiiiiiiii!" Alison said, and gave him a ridiculous hug that hurt his shoulders.

Brad was now being managed.

Alison's office was small, but it was definitely there, with a door that closed, off an enormous bullpen of hustling young people, all of whom looked at Brad with a weird mixture of loathing, suspicion, envy, and pity. She introduced Brad around. "Nice to meet you," Brad was soon to learn, was the phrase in Hollywood you could trust second least, right after "I'm a big fan."

"I'm a big fan," Alison said to Brad as he sat down in an uncomfortable plastic chair on the other side of her desk. The office was decorated with three movie posters, one for a movie that Brad had actually seen, and an old head shot of Johnny Depp, autographed with a black lip-print. Alison also had a shelf of books, mostly low-end sci-fi and thrillers, which Brad assumed were part of her current client list. Obviously Alison wasn't repping Stephen King or Neil Gaiman, but she was clearly at least in the game. It didn't take a whole hell of a lot to be considered legit in LA. In the parlance of the town, it was an honor to be nominated.

"I have some plans for you," Alison said. "Assuming we're going to be working together from now on. Are we?"

"Sure," Brad said, sealing himself into the tomb.

"First, we need to send you around town to get people used to the idea of you."

"I didn't know there *was* an idea of me."

"You're funny," she said. "I've been making some calls, and people love the sound of your book. I just want to put you in some rooms and see if you connect with anyone."

That, Brad soon learned, was the essence of the entertainment industry, an endlessly neurotic blind date arranged by an ever-shifting army of 10 percent yentas. He stayed in LA for a week and took forty meetings, including one with two men wearing identical navy blazers who had an office decorated with no less than seventeen African rubber plants, and one in a back office on the Warner Brothers lot with an impossibly tan guy whose eyes were wider than a five-year-old girl's at a pony farm. The guy wore a bright pink Izod golf shirt with the collar up and told Brad that Matthew Perry really loves science fiction. Brad also met with one of the creators of *Frasier*, who was busy practicing his golf swing in the office. They made small talk for five minutes and then the guy said, refreshingly, "So why the fuck are you here, you idiot?"

"I have no idea," Brad said. "I just go where they tell me."

The guy laughed and gave Brad the week's only truly genuine handshake. Brad never saw him again.

He drove from Culver City up to Burbank and down to Santa Monica and then back to Universal City and across the Cahuenga Pass many times, until the backseat of his car was a pungent mess of In-N-Out Burger bags and taco wrappers, and he was very glad he'd rented a relatively fuel-efficient car.

It was actually sort of incredible. He'd drive onto the lot of a movie studio, a place where they *actually made movies*, and would show a security guard his driver's license. The guards checked their lists and asked, "Do you know where you're going?" When Brad said no, they gave him a map and said, "They're expecting you." Then he'd go to a windowless office and someone about his age would give him a bottle of water, and then he'd have a chat with someone older than him, more than one of whom said "Alison knows a lot of people and has good taste," and then he'd run to the bathroom and pee out the entire bottle of water, drive ten miles in one hour, and repeat the process. The sun felt so warm on his face all day.

Brad once had cared about what was going on in the country and the wider world. He had aspired to be a serious person. But no more. This seemed like a nicer life. LA had weaved its dumbass spell over him.

One night, far too late, he said to his wife on the phone, "I went to a bar and this guy from *Mr. Show* was playing the piano."

"What's *Mr. Show*?" she said.

Brad went home to Chicago and froze his ass for two months. One night he and Juliet went to a Colombian steakhouse on Lincoln Avenue to celebrate their first anniversary. They ordered the *matrimonio*, an incredibly delicious mixed grill of steak and shrimp served with grilled taro root and a side of homemade *chimichurri* and were happily in the middle of their second bottle of wine when Brad's black Nokia phone, which he'd purchased reluctantly two months earlier, rang. The phone looked like a turd with a punch pad and a stubby penis antenna, but it had cool interchangeable faceplates and was proving increasingly useful. The LED readout showed an LA number.

"You mind if I take this?" he asked Juliet.

She waved him on, her mouth full of steak.

It was Alison Shreveport. "How's it going, Brad?" she asked.

"It's my anniversary and I'm out for dinner."

"CONGRATULATIONS!!!!!" she said, far too enthusiastically. "I was married once, but he was a crackhead, so we had to sell the house."

"Oh."

"So I have some exciting news," Alison said.

"Yes?"

"Someone wants to option *Going Nuclear*."

"Really?"

"Yes. He was a producer at Warner Brothers, but then he had an overall at Universal and also one at DreamWorks, but now he's on his own but has a golden parachute at both places."

Brad had no idea what any of that meant, but he did sort of understand.

"He loves your book and is willing to give you seventy-five for it."

"Seventy-five dollars?" Brad asked. "That's not enough."

"No," Alison said. "Seventy-five *thousand* dollars."

"*What?*"

"We'll see if we can give you first crack at the screenplay so I can get you into the Writers Guild. They have excellent health insurance."

"You're not playing a joke on me?"

"No, this actually happens to people sometimes."

"Do . . . do you need me out there?"

"It wouldn't hurt," Alison said.

"Am I supposed to thank you?"

"That's generally considered good manners."

And so Brad did, for several minutes. By the time he got back, his half of the *matrimonio* was cold, and Juliet was looking annoyed.

"That better have been very important," she said.

"It was," he said.

Brad sat in silence for several seconds, staring at a pile of shrimp shells.

"*What*, dude?" said his wife.

"We have to move to Los Angeles," he said.

By that summer, they were there, living in an apartment in a scary white concrete building near Hollywood and Vine. The place had two stories, both of them completely disgusting, and it was kind of expensive, which meant they began to chew through their modest savings. Eventually Brad got his deal and his script, so they had a little bit more money, plus health insurance, which was good because Juliet got pregnant.

They moved to a dumpy house in a pretty nice neighborhood, but then the script money started to run out too, so they moved to a slightly nicer house in a not-as-nice neighborhood. *Going Nuclear*, both the script and the option, went into turnaround, and soon the book was forgotten and Juliet was pregnant again. Brad got a job as a staff writer on a Canadian cartoon called *Battlecats*, which ran at 3:30 p.m. weekdays on the WB affiliate and featured a weird live-action turn by a Hungarian movie star playing the Clawmaster, the Battlecats' archenemy, an evil half-cat, half-man druid who lived with a trio of goblin puppets in what looked like the basement of a steampunk distillery. It was a reboot of a franchise that had been popular in the '80s, but the second go-around didn't quite capture the cheesy magic of the original.

After twenty-five dreary *Battlecats* episodes, Brad returned to his regularly scheduled program of driving around to meetings with people he'd never see again at companies that didn't really exist. He smoked a lot of pot for inspiration and sold one other spec script, which never got made. In all, he earned about $300,000, which sounds like a lot of money and would be a lot of money under normal circumstances, but it's not really that much when you spread it over ten years, give 15 percent of it to lawyers and are trying to support a family of four in Los Angeles. Maybe they shouldn't have bought that Prius in 2007, but it was hard to resist the gas mileage, and it's not like they'd bitten on the premium package. Regardless, a decade had passed since they moved to LA, and with it another semipromising literary career dried out under the Southern California sun, like so many kale chips in an oven preheated to four hundred degrees.

It should have gone so much better, he thought to himself, as he did every morning.

And with that it was time for Brad Cohen to face his present-day reality. Brad sighed and stood up, his belly hanging farther over his plaid pajama bottoms than he would have liked. Last night's massive weed session to coincide with the Lakers-Spurs game had left his brain and lungs feeling gummy. People told him that vaporizing was supposed to be better for him than smoking, but he'd yet to feel the evidence. Maybe he should stop with the pot. But then he wouldn't be able to get stoned anymore, and that was hardly a solution.

Brad went to the bedroom door, which was as shitty and disgusting as ever. Kedzie, the dog, clawed at it with dirty paws every morning at six, so it looked like the dog had been rubbing his ass up against it for a decade. What had once been at least part of a tree was now a dog-shit door. To Brad, that pretty much summed it up.

He'd always imagined that his adult home would be a prideful thing, a personal-taste fiefdom of lacquered floors and handmade art and shiny, humming, energy-efficient appliances, a fire in the hearth, a driveway that didn't buckle, high-beamed ceilings, and speakers built into the media-room wall. People would come over and he'd grill meat and they'd admire the color of his den. But no one ever came over, because there was no place to sit. His house had dust bunnies in the corners, mold in the kitchen caulking, weird splotches on the hall floors, yard-sale dining room chairs, and a rusty hinge on the backyard shed. The light in the bedroom closet had shorted out years ago. He kept his sweaters from the '90s in a kitchen drawer, under the strainers and the cheese grater. There was no other space. Plus, he didn't even own the house. But he had an Xbox 360. That was something.

Juliet sat on the couch with Cori, the four-year-old. Claire, the seven-year-old, had been carpooled away hours ago to the extremely mediocre neighborhood public school, where the classroom wall art looked like it had been produced in the fatal-disease ward at the children's hospital. This is where Brad would send his beautiful girls for years so that they could gradually have their winning, innocent spirits sucked from their bodies.

He'd always wanted two girls named Mary and Rhoda. Juliet nixed that, and *especially* nixed his next suggestion, Maude and Rhoda. From there the suggestions got progressively worse. After Juliet said no to George and Weezie, and Brad had said no to Thelma and Louise, they'd decided to name their kids as the kids arrived.

Juliet and Cori were watching *Yo Gabba Gabba!* Everyone he knew seemed to love that show, but Brad hated it so much. *Your time to rock has ended, Gen X*, he thought. *No beatboxing mack daddy in a puffy, multicolored Kroft hat is ever going to bring back your youth.* Or maybe he was just envious of the creators. He felt that way about most people his age who were more successful than he was. Regardless, the show was hyper and shrill and annoying. It really frosted his donut.

"Turn that crap off," he said.

"Look, honey," said Juliet. "Daddy's awake!"

Cori, wearing a purple tutu and as adorable as a Muppet, bounded off the couch and gave Brad a big hug.

"You smell pretty bad, Daddy," she said.

"Don't I know it," he said.

———

They got Cori to sit at a table in her room with some crayons and a little plastic dish of baby carrots. She'd stay reliably quiet for twenty minutes that way, maybe even a half hour, which her beleaguered parents immeasurably appreciated. It was a big difference from Claire, who talked constantly and required entertainment from the moment she awoke until the moment the melatonin finally kicked in and she mercifully went to sleep, often not until after nine thirty. Cori, on the other hand, could stare at a ladybug half the day and not even notice that she had to pee, which created its own disruptions but was less obtrusive in the main.

This allowed Brad some minutes to sit at the table with a cup of strong tea and a bowl of granola, which Juliet had made, smothered in almond milk, which she hadn't made but had persuaded him to use instead of regular milk, which bloated his stomach and made his face blotchy. His wife sat across from him, smiling. How he admired her. Unlike Brad, who most days looked and felt like something left out beside the recycling can, Juliet hadn't even been remotely ravaged by middle age's silent, relentless creep. True, she wasn't one of these LA women whom motherhood had somehow made thinner, blonder, and tanner; their family didn't have the resources for that level of beauty bionics. The births had broadened her hips, and the lugging around of kids and their crap gear had done the same to her shoulders. But her skin still shone vitally, her eyes were white and clear. Her hair, maybe a little gray around the edges, had texture and substance. She was so beautiful. The world hadn't beaten Juliet.

Here was her secret: herbs. She'd never had much of a career. When Brad had met her, she'd been working at the gift shop of the Art Institute and selling hand-knitted blankets at the occasional Lincoln Park craft market. After they'd moved to California, she'd made a couple of half-hearted attempts at being a personal assistant, but she wasn't that good at the gig, and then the kids came along and they couldn't afford day care. But she grew the herbs like weeds, which some of them technically were. The house's only successful feature was a sunroom in the front, which mostly had glass walls and got great light all day. That, along with a corner of the backyard where the dog wasn't permitted to roam, was where Juliet put her pots and planters, filled with the secrets of the forest and the jungle. You had your literal garden-variety basils and tarragons, thyme and oregano, all of which made the food taste really good. But Juliet's real gift was for the medicinal stuff, obscure mosses and worts, damiana and various salvias. She had cone plants and succulents and fragrants that, if not cooked in just the right way, could be fatal if ingested. These she kept on a shelf so high that even the cat couldn't access them.

Juliet stewed her herbs. Some of them she froze. She made them into sprays and tinctures, salves and ointments, combining them with root essences that she'd bought at an Asian specialty store in Alhambra. She put them into bottles and jars, plugged them with corks and rubber stoppers, and made her own labels. The only herb she didn't traffic in was the one Brad desired most, but he had a prescription that he could cash in for that at an infinite number of stores around town. There were other plants, other remedies, and Juliet made hundreds of dollars a month selling them online, sometimes for as much as $1,500 during prime allergy season. That money had made a huge difference lately. The *Battlecats* residual checks were getting smaller and smaller.

One night, as Juliet stood at the stove stewing up a semifoul, greenish-black concoction in a copper pot, she wore a flowing, gray pashmina knockoff. The cat perched on her shoulder. As he watched the steam billow about Juliet's face, Brad had a somewhat stunning thought: *My wife is a witch.*

She wasn't an Elizabeth Montgomery or Melissa Joan Hart kind of witch who could wriggle her nose and then suddenly his boss (not that he *had* a boss, goddammit) would be standing there in his underwear holding a cocktail shaker. She wasn't a Witch of Eastwick or some kind of hot Fairuza Balk–like goth chick either. This wasn't *Charmed*. But Brad's kitchen definitely hosted some kind of daily witchcraft.

Later, after the kids were asleep, he confronted her. "You're a witch," he said.

"What are you talking about?"

"Admit it."

"*I not*," she said, which is how their baby had always said it.

"You make *potions*," he said. "Every night. You put roots into a cauldron while you're singing."

Juliet blushed, as though she'd been caught doing something shameful.

"Look," she said, "I'm not interested in casting a circle, like all those people I follow on Facebook. I don't want to learn *spells*. But I do believe that the earth contains ancient healing properties, and I want to tap into that tradition."

"It's OK, dude," Brad said. "I don't care that you're a witch. You do a good job."

"Thank you, honey," she said.

"I think you're a sexy witch."

"It's not about being sexy. It's about having a profound connection to the earth."

"I understand," he said, hoping to steer her away from politics tonight.

"This is about physical and psychological healing. People can sniff out phony witches from a long way off."

"I imagine that's true," he said, "but can you use witchcraft to manipulate me sexually, you sexy witch?"

"Stop with the sex," she said.

He gave her the pouty smile he knew she couldn't resist. She smiled back.

"We can try a few things," she said.

Many happy months followed.

Brad liked Juliet's witchery, especially because she was so circumspect about it in public. It was almost like a secret identity. Besides him, only the fellow members of her "witch group," as she now allowed herself to call it, knew. "Isn't that called a coven?" he'd asked, but she'd scolded him for being so recherché.

In any case: witch.

Now that he knew her secret, it was all she'd ever talk about at home. As they sat there at the breakfast table, precious child-free seconds ticking away, she described how a rival witch group, which was far more committed to goddess worship than hers, was trying to take away their Sunday meeting space at the nearby Unitarian church by offering the congregation more money. Apparently, witch factions didn't coexist well in the same space, and making things more complicated was the fact that a group of male witches, largely interested in the sexual powers of black magic, had begun to occasionally troll the witch group's Facebook page, bringing foul, corruptive, sexist talk to innocent exchanges about herbal efficacy.

"Wow, the Wiccan world is so political," Brad said.

"We're not Wiccan, technically," said Juliet. "But yeah, you have no idea."

The little one approached the table. "I threw up," she said.

Brad rolled his eyes. That girl vomited more than Caligula.

"Well, we should clean you, then," Juliet said.

"I need to get clean myself," Brad said. "I have a pitch meeting today."

"You do? With you?"

"Fox. The drama people. Alison set it up."

"That's a big deal. Why didn't you tell me?"

He hadn't told her because he'd almost forgotten. A decade of driving into the void will do that to you. The idea of going to Hollywood and talking about your ideas to TV and movie producers sounds glamorous. And it is, if you actually sell any of those ideas. If you don't, then you're little better than someone going door to door selling carpet samples, or working the diet-powder table at Costco, except that those people occasionally make a sale.

Amazingly, Brad had never been on a film or TV set, had never seen a camera roll. Raymond Chandler once said that you could live your whole life in Hollywood and never get to the part where they make the movies, and he was right. *Battlecats* didn't count because they animated it in Croatia and did the soundstage crap in Toronto.

The traditional LA arc is all about the crack-up, the meteor shot to success gradually frittered away by a lifetime of bad luck, bad decisions, and bad drugs. The grocery stores of Sherman Oaks are littered with such cases. And then you have the people who play it right—more than you might imagine, actually—who make good connections and good money and work hard enough and long enough to carry themselves through to retiring in Ojai. Those are the people Brad envied most, the ones who'd never really accomplished anything but still had private orange groves on their property. J. J. Abrams was a faraway dream. Brad knew he didn't have those chops and never would.

His ambitions didn't exactly soar anymore. Brad didn't dream of being the editor of the *New Century*. Even publishing another book was beyond him now. But that guy who'd worked a few seasons on the *Lost* staff and then had a couple of fantasy scripts on the Black List? Brad could have been that guy. Two seasons, maybe three, on *The Mentalist* was all he asked. If asked, he'd have agreed to do that job. But there were a lot of people in line who were better connected and more talented than he'd ever been. No one was going to ask.

He got into the shower. Whenever he was feeling OK about his life, all he had to do was shower, and that disabused him of any optimism. It wasn't a nice shower—at all. The landlady had converted the garage more than a decade ago, adding a bathroom. But she'd either done all the work herself, or she'd hired the Three Stooges. The stall had been unevenly tiled. Bulbous chunks of brown paste clumped in the corners, making the floor almost impossible to clean and permanently moldy. The wall tile was no better, with light brown smears all over, and squares that bulged out at odd angles. The water pressure was so strong, so sharp, and the temperature so erratic that it felt to Brad like guards were hosing him down. To add to the ambience, the landlady hadn't put a light in over the stall, and the room had no windows. It was like showering in a dark cage. He found himself longing to spend the night in a motel just so he could take a bath in a cheap plastic tub. That would have been the Chateau Marmont by comparison.

On the floor sat two drains, inexplicably side by side, with checked metal covers. When you removed the covers, you saw nothing but a hole opening into the ground. Brad wondered where the wastewater actually went. Did it just gather in puddles underneath the house? If he took a shit down the hole, would it just drop straight into the sewer? He never did, but he was tempted.

Many mornings he'd spend wasted minutes in the stall, using more water than he should, slapping his head against the slimy tile or haphazardly scraping mold off the clear plastic curtain with his fingernail. *The shower should be a nice time*, he thought. *Why is the shower not a nice time?*

On that morning, as he rinsed himself for another trip into the void, Brad knew: he was a failure.

You only get one chance in this life. His career browser couldn't be refreshed. Brad was just about out of dimes for the meter.

After fifteen totally wasteful minutes of water torture, he got out, dried himself, and put on a clean pair of dark Old Navy jeans and a cherry-red Penguin golf shirt that had looked very fashionable when he'd seen Adam Brody wear it on *The O.C.* seven years ago. The shirt had faded a bit, and the collar was fraying, but it still fit, so Brad kept it in the rotation. New clothes for Daddy weren't exactly in the budget these days.

Once more unto the breach.

———

Before his meeting, Brad met his manager at John O'Groats on West Pico. It had blue-and-white-checked tablecloths and maps of Scotland on the wall. There were little dishes of caramelized apples on the table so that you could scoop them into your Dutch baby pancake after you punctured the dough. This was what frustrated Brad about LA the most: you had all these incredible places to eat and drink, and lots of weird old stores full of character and characters, and then you headed out into the belly of the day, and the city seemed to be composed of nothing but guys with leaf blowers and horrible plastic people who were out to ruin your career. So a diner like this one served as both an oasis and a mirage.

Brad got to the restaurant late, after driving around for twenty minutes looking for a free place to park. Alison was sitting at a table, talking on her smartphone. She waved him over and mouthed the words "Just a second," and then proceeded with her conversation, which seemed to consist of the word "OK" twenty times, followed by a loud, "Well then you can go fucking screw yourself!" And then she hung up.

"Sorry," she said. "My nanny's being a real pain in the ass."

"Sure," Brad said.

The decade since Brad moved to town, which felt like a century, had been hard on Alison as well. She'd quit the Film Strip a couple years after he'd arrived, much to his worry, but had quickly signed on at another company that appeared to have almost identical offices. There had been several changes since then, including a few distressing months where she'd set up a desk in a corner of the communal gym in a condo complex where she didn't even live. Brad could barely hear her over the endless whirl of the elliptical trainers. Currently she was working solo out of a room on the seventh floor of a high-rise in Century City but seemed to be doing well enough so that she could afford to pay someone to handle her e-mail. In the meantime she'd adopted a preteen Guatemalan orphan, who was giving her all kinds of problems.

"My Producers Guild insurance doesn't cover speech therapy," she said. "Can you believe that?"

"Crazy," Brad said.

His own insurance had run out three years previous, and now he just paid out the hole for catastrophic coverage for the girls. The rest of their health care was in his witchy wife's hands. She was doing a good job so far, but he always worried.

He complained about that for a few minutes. Alison poked away at her phone, not even feigning interest.

"Sorry," she said. "Trying to arrange something for later."

"Of course," Brad said.

He wondered if this relationship, the longest single one of his professional career, still had legs, or even thighs. Alison seemed to have lost interest in him around the time of *Battlecats*. He'd brought up this disinterest to her many times. "I can't sell you if you don't give me anything to sell," she always said. Maybe he was hoping for too much. The idea that you could fall upward professionally in this town without actually working might have been a myth.

"So what have you got for Fox today?" she said.

"I think it's a really strong idea," he said.

But it was a really weak idea. In fact, calling it an idea at all would be giving it too much credit. When Brad had started, he'd go into pitch meetings *prepared*, with twelve-page dossiers on each character, season arcs, episode outlines, a universe of possibilities exploding inside his head. He'd talk for a half hour, occasionally answer some questions, and then ten days later Alison would call him and say, "It's not quite what the network is looking for." Then two years later a much worse version of what he'd proposed would appear on the network, making him think that it was all just a big fat fucking lie. So he stopped trying.

"Good," she said. "I had to pull a lot of strings to get you this meeting."

You did not, Brad thought. That's all these people did all day: sit in rooms and listen to pitches from fat, desperate hacks for TV shows that would never get made by anyone anywhere. Sure, not everyone in the world could get a development meeting, but once you were in the system, you had to really work hard to get completely expunged, like a washed-up veteran ballplayer who gets a spring-training invite out of courtesy.

Sometimes Brad wondered what it'd be like to be on the other side of the ledger. It wasn't a job he wanted really. But hypocritical, mendacious, and shallow as development work was, it at least qualified as steady pay. For once he wanted to be the one passing judgment. Then he hated himself for that thought. People built skyscrapers every day. They were transforming the world by their thoughts and deeds, and working for President Obama. The current editor of the *New Century* was ten years younger than he was and appeared on MSNBC almost every day. There was plenty of envy to go around. But Hollywood had limited Brad's perspective. He was now officially envious of junior-level network TV development executives. He wanted whatever they had.

"I won't let you down," he said, though he probably would.

Their food came. Alison picked at a Greek salad while Brad snarfed his French dip with fries way too quickly.

"This is my last lunch in my thirties," he said.

"On my fortieth birthday," Alison said, "I learned that it's really hard to OD on rum. But I managed to do it."

She always made Brad feel better about himself, which is why he still kept her on retainer. He wasn't quite sure why she returned the favor. After all, 10 percent of zero is zero.

Alison paid, a merciful act, and then she said, "You want to follow me over there?"

"Why don't we just walk?" Brad said. "It's only three blocks."

"*Really?*" she said.

"Sure."

"They don't let you onto the lot if you don't drive," she said.

"Fine," Brad said.

They went outside. A weather pattern had begun to brew. The sky grayed rapidly, filling with strange, cloudy swirls interspersed with riveting cones of light, as though heaven were playing favorites with certain street corners. A gust of wind smacked the restaurant awning. Fat vortices of grit and garbage updrafted the breadth of Pico. Brad looked at the weather app on his phone. A High Wind Advisory was in effect for LA and surrounding counties. Was a hard rain gonna fall too?

Brad raised his fists to the sky. "Why do you mock me, God?" he cried.

Alison looked at him with pity. "You want me to give you a ride?" she said. "My car's nicer than yours."

Wasn't everyone's?

———

They parked in Lot C, a spot marked "TV Visitor." The wind had reached sandstorm levels. It howled ominously through the garage slats, setting off car alarms. Brad and Alison escaped into a glass walkway, plastered with cartoon images to promote the new season of *Family Guy*. It swayed and rattled in the wind like a covered bridge above a gorge.

An endless series of elevators and hallways followed, all of them adorned with wall-length posters of TV shows that Brad either hadn't seen or absolutely hated. Why was he even doing this? He didn't like TV, except for *Mad Men* and sometimes *30 Rock*. He would have liked to be involved in making those shows. But he might as well have said, "I would like to help God make the oceans."

More than any of the other networks, Fox liked to ritually humiliate its show prospectors. CBS and ABC, which comprised the 2010 top tier, offered executive-class seating, up-to-date trade mags to read, and complimentary tea and coffee. NBC, still praying for the return of the Friends, had cheap plastic seats and neon piping, a doctor's office in desperate need of a refresh, but you got the sense that they'd pamper their clients if they could afford to do so. Fox, on the other hand, despite having the deep pockets of a major corporation behind it, not to mention the endless millions of *The Simpsons* and *Family Guy*, liked to run its development offices like a frat house. That's how Brad found himself sitting in a pounded-out beanbag chair, reading an old issue of *Vice*. He wondered if he'd ever be able to stand up. It felt like someone was running a belt sander across his sacrum.

Alison stood next to him, texting furiously.

"The pool man forgot where I keep the key to the back gate," she said.

"Right," he said.

Brad wondered what it would be like to have a pool man. Sometimes when his parents came to town, they stayed at a hotel with a pool, and occasionally he and Juliet would go to a pool party at the house of someone whose success they resented. Other than that, there were no pools in Brad's life. More troubling, though, was his realization that he'd never even seen Alison's house. He didn't know where she lived, or with whom, other than her troubled adoptee. She'd been married about five years ago, but that status could easily have changed by now. How could the most important person in his career operate under such a veil of inscrutability? He was staggered daily by just how little control he had over his own life.

An assistant, somewhere between twenty-two years old and total asshole, appeared with a clipboard.

"Sorry to keep you waiting," she said. "The last meeting is running a little bit long. Can I get you some water?"

That was how the networks kept people in their places: making sure that by the time the meeting started, you had to pee so badly you couldn't think. Everything was designed specifically to knock down the king's petitioners. With so many millions at stake, the networks couldn't afford to deal with uppity bottom-feeders.

Brad chewed at his fingers nervously. It was bad enough going into these meetings prepared. But this time he had nothing, and he wasn't sure if he was going to be able to bluff.

Finally the time arrived. They got walked down a row of cubicles, occupied by another platoon of keyboard-clacking, noise-reduction-headphones-wearing entertainment-industry drones. These young people, who spent all day in a soulless office surrounded by cartoon swag, had no idea how fortunate they were. All around, windows rattled. Brad could see palm trees bending.

Harsh winds indeed.

The assistant took Brad and Alison into a conference room, which was enclosed by glass on all sides. The pitches the network actually wanted to consider took place in plush offices on another floor. This was where executives held the "courtesy meetings." It was a simulacrum of business, an illusion worthy of the opening reel of *The Matrix*. Brad sat down in an uncomfortable soft-backed office chair, one of dozens around an oblong plastic table. In front of each chair sat a phone with speakers sprouting from either side. Brad wondered if they were actually even connected to anything. He'd been doing this for a decade. Never once had anyone conferenced into a meeting.

"They'll be right in," the assistant said.

Brad nodded. Alison didn't look up from her phone. She seemed to be smiling as she typed. Brad wondered if she was having an affair with the pool man, or maybe "pool man" was just a euphemism for something else, like "man who hung around the pool all day waiting for you to come home from work." He wouldn't put that beyond her reach. There were certainly people in LA who spent their days that way.

The door opened. Executives entered. Alison activated.

"Hiiiiiiiiii!" she exclaimed.

The executives looked at her coldly. Brad realized that she didn't know them. He wasn't much surprised.

"Thank you for coming in," one of them said.

They all shook hands. Brad had never seen two of them before. The roster was always changing. He no longer even bothered to learn their names.

"Sure!" Alison said. "We're very excited. You know Brad."

The third executive gave him a look that shriveled Brad's heart.

"Oh yes," he said. "I know Brad."

Trey Peters. Brad had been dealing with him for a decade. They'd never had any kind of exchange outside these meetings, via e-mail or anything else, and yet this guy clearly despised him, as he despised everyone. The smug bastard just moved from network to network, rejecting people's dreams. Not that he had any green-lighting power; the decisions all got made two levels above him. Peters was just the guy who pulled the lever on the electric chair. If you had to meet with him, you were already dead.

Outside the glass-walled room, Brad noticed, young people were gathering, holding tablets like interns at an operating theater. If you wanted to learn how to eviscerate properly, you needed to watch. And since the meetings were also available to hear on an office-wide intercom system, you could listen as well.

The executives sat across the table from Brad and Alison and crossed their hands, as if to say, *We cannot be impressed.*

"Well," Alison, "for those of you who don't know Brad, he wrote one of my *favorite* novels of all time, *Going Postal.*"

"*Going Nuclear,*" Brad said.

"Right," Alison said. "Well, it came out a long time ago."

Brad felt a little twist of the knife. Alison didn't like getting shown up.

"*And since then,*" Alison said, "he's been working on various TV shows and movies."

"Which ones, Brad?" said Trey Peters. "Not everyone in here is as familiar with your work as I am."

You bastard, Brad thought.

"*Battlecats,*" Brad said very softly.

"I'm sorry, what was that?" said Trey.

"*Battlecats,*" said Brad louder.

"Oh," said Trey. "*Battlecats.*"

"So tell us about your current project, Brad," said one of the other executives.

"Well, it's a TV show," Brad said.

"How convenient!" Trey said. "We *make* TV shows here."

The other executives laughed too loudly. Brad even heard laughter from outside the glass walls. He began to sweat.

"I really think it could be a new *X-Files* for you," Brad said.

"*The X-Files?*" said Tripp.

"Yeah."

"That went off the air eight years ago. We're not really looking for a new one."

"OK, well, my idea stands by itself too."

"That's good to know."

"So the main character is a guy."

"A guy, Brad? He is a *guy like you*?"

It was liked being heckled by an ornery DA. Alison wasn't paying attention, so there was no one to object on Brad's behalf, and there certainly wasn't a judge in the room. Unless that judge was Trey.

"Well," Brad said, "he's kind of an everyman."

"OK, so not like you then."

Dick.

"So what happens to this everyman?" asked another one of the executives, who was either dumb or trying to be nice or both.

"He gets caught in an infinite time loop," Brad said.

"A what?"

"An infinite time loop."

"What's that?"

"Well, it's a loop in time. And it goes on infinitely."

"But how does it work?"

"It's kind of hard to explain."

"Go on, Brad," said Trey. "*Explain.*"

"Well, so, he's a guy."

"You said that already."

"And time keeps looping around him."

"Right."

"So he keeps on having the same experiences over and over again."

"How so?"

"He's caught in a loop."

"The same experiences, though? Wouldn't that get boring?"

"He's trying to find out what happened to him and trying to get out of the loop."

"You mean like *Groundhog Day*?"

"No, that's a comedy. And it takes place over the course of just one day. This is more of a mystery sci-fi thriller. Almost a *Twilight Zone*–like anthology show, but about one guy's life. There would be stand-alone plots but also this through line where he tries to figure out what's happening to him and why."

Alison had stopped texting and was now looking at him with something vaguely close to interest on her face. The more Brad talked about this idea, the better it seemed to him. Networks put stupider stuff than that on TV every year.

"OK," Trey said.

That wasn't exactly enthusiasm, but it wasn't mockery either. Brad wanted nothing else from these meetings. He'd always thought that if they'd stop making fun of him for just a second and let him explain, he might be able to come up with something good. And now they were going to let him.

This would be the moment that he transformed from Brad Cohen, Hollywood hack, into Brad Cohen, acclaimed showrunner. The next time he went to Comic-Con, it wouldn't be as a fan or a cosplay enthusiast. He'd be all-access, a panelist. He'd never have to drive himself to San Diego again.

"So . . ." Brad said.

A shrill whooping noise went off, vibrating the room's glass walls. It was punctuated by three long, discordant honks. Red lights began to flash everywhere. The woman who'd escorted them into the room burst in, looking a little scared.

"That windstorm is whipping electrical wires all over the place," she said. "They're saying it's a severe fire risk and that we have to evacuate the building immediately."

Whoooooooop! Whoooooooop! Whoooooooop! went the alarm. *Hawnk! Hawnk! Hawnk!*

Alison said, "Well, maybe we should table this until—"

Hawnk! Hawnk! Hawnk!

Trey's eyes filled with evil intent.

"Keep pitching," he said.

"But Trey," said one of the other executives, "we have to evacuate."

"We will," Trey said. "But I really want to hear what Brad has to say."

"I don't think—" said Brad.

"Keep pitching!"

Brad sighed. "OK," he said. "So in each episode, the infinite time loop takes him to another place in his life, where he has to decide—"

Hawnk! Hawnk! Hawnk!

A window shattered, and someone screamed. The junior executives began to look really nervous.

"Trey, I really don't think—"

"No," said Trey Peters. "We are going to finish this pitch meeting. I really want to hear what Brad Cohen has to say for himself because I admired his work on *Battlecats* so much."

"He has to decide," Brad said, "what to do in that moment and how to find his way out."

Whooooooop! Whoooooop! Whoooooooop!

Outside the conference room, young people who'd never experienced this level of terror outside of a *Paranormal Activity* screening were grabbing whatever personal electronic devices they could find and running around like frightened bunnies. Drops of rain the size of stinkbugs splattered the windows. It was as though Roland Emmerich were directing the day.

Now the alarms wouldn't stop. The air filled with an endless *hawnking*, and Trey Peters finally threw up his hands. "Fine," he said. "Brad, you can finish tomorrow."

"I'll call you to schedule him in," Alison said.

"Who are you again?" Trey asked her.

Brad and Alison fled the meeting with something close to enthusiasm, clutching their shoulder bags like wealthy women walking through an alley. The building was filled with panicked people who earned their livings not returning phone calls until 6:30 p.m. There was no way out but the glass walkway, which shimmered with water like it was the central tunnel of a car wash. Brad could hear the hot, beautiful banshee wind outside.

The garage floor was wet, as though a river had just overrun its banks. They got inside Alison's Lexus SUV. Brad was relieved to smell the leather. He exhaled.

"Well, that was bad luck, huh?" he said.

Alison looked at him sternly.

"Is something wrong?" he said.

"That was so awful, Brad," she said.

"I know, right?" he said. "'Keep pitching.' What an asshole."

"No, I mean the pitch itself. A guy caught in an infinite time loop. What kind of fucking bullshit are you trying to sell?"

"But—"

"You need to lay off the pot," she said. "It's making you soft and stupid."

"But the pot is the only thing that gives my life *meaning*," he said.

That was only half-true, but he was sorry he'd said it. He also wanted to say, "Well, you haven't been much help, you know," but he didn't like confrontation.

"Pathetic," she said. "You've been a great disappointment to me in many ways."

"I'm sorry," he said.

"Don't be sorry," she said. "Drop your cocks and grab your socks."

"What does that mean?"

"It means get back to work."

"But I have nothing to say."

Alison regarded him scornfully. "Someone once told me that Brad Cohen will be the best thing that ever happens to your career," she said. "But it hasn't really worked out that way."

"For either of us," Brad said.

She drove him back to his car in disapproving silence.

By the time Brad began his journey home, the rain had stopped, and by the time he got halfway, there were rainbows over Griffith Park. Two years hence they would have been the most Instagrammed rainbows of all time, but for now, in the common era before infinitely shared online photography, they just existed as reminders that there was something beyond all this.

You put in the days, Brad thought. *You put in the hours. You try.* But he had even disappointed Alison. Talk about not clearing a low bar.

He parked the Prius on lower Sunset, two doors down from the Green Athena. The city kept shutting down his favorite dispensaries, but this one was pretty good so far. There was a courtyard with a fountain and a smoking table, and they always banged a gong when a customer entered. It was a lot better than the one behind Burrito King on Hyperion, which had anarchist pamphlets scattered around and scary dogs that barked at you while you examined the wares. Of course, the fountain at Green Athena wasn't working, and the bottom had grown thick with algae, but Brad's expectations where pretty low for a quasi-legal marijuana shop in Echo Park.

At the entrance sat a thick-necked cholo wearing a gun holster.

"ID," he said with understandable resentment. If he'd ever got caught with as much weed as he saw white dudes walk out of here with, he'd be doing five to ten in San Quentin, no questions. One man's medicine was another man's doom. But Brad couldn't worry about that right now. He'd printed out an Internet coupon for thirty-five dollars an eighth.

Green Athena had a good selection. Brad stuck his nose in a jar of Tangerine Dream and also one of Orange You Glad. In general, he only consumed strains that were named after citrus fruits. Anything indica brought him down. One time he'd smoked a bowl of Chronic Grape Kush and wanted to saw off his arm. The only worse strain he'd ever experienced had been called Walter Mondale. He didn't have much wisdom to pass down to his daughters, but "Don't buy ironically named pot" was definitely on the list.

Finally, Brad settled on an eighth of Lemon Lift.

"That's a good one," said the cute girl behind the counter, though she said that to every customer.

"Well, it's my birthday tomorrow, so I thought I'd treat myself."

The girl cocked her head so cutely, in a manner clearly learned by watching the early performances of Zooey Deschanel.

"Awwwww," she said. "Happy birthday!"

"Thanks," Brad said.

"How old are you?"

"Forty."

"God," she said. "I'm so sorry."

"It happens to everybody," said Brad.

"I hope it never happens to me," said the girl.

She weighed out Brad's order and then gave him a little extra with a wink. He paid. She slid a fat joint into a paper bag.

"It's a present from us," she said.

"Is it sativa?" he said.

"It's a blend," she said. "Mostly shake."

Brad appreciated her generosity but knew that if he smoked the wrong stuff, it could really mess up his brain. He was forty now, basically, and he had to be careful. But when he walked outside, the sun had come out and the air was crisp and cleanly breathable, as it always is the first hour after an LA rain. Suddenly the day seemed possible again.

The patio table was still soaked, so he sparked up standing, his face instantly enveloped in a cloud of smoke. The weed tasted fragrant and good. He smoked it down to the nub, putting the roach in the key pocket of his jeans for later. It didn't occur to him until he got into the car that he'd have to drive home stoned.

By the time Brad reached the highway 2 on-ramp, his legs felt leaden, and his brain felt like a mash. The road seemed to come up at him in 3-D. Whoa. NPR sounded distant, as though it were being broadcasted in from a faraway star, a soothing, disconnected buzz.

Don't drive stoned, Cohen, he said to himself. The phrase echoed around in his head like a squash ball going back and forth in an empty court. But somehow he made it up the hills and pulled into his cracked driveway still breathing.

Brad went inside. His girls were there, watching TV and eating chocolate ice cream. Juliet stood in the kitchen, stewing herbs. Cori and Claire shouted his name and ran up to hug him. He hugged them back.

"You guys are Ewoks," he said spacily.

"Daddy's home!" Juliet said.

She came over, gave him a kiss, and wrinkled her nose.

"Ooooh," Juliet said to the girls passive-aggressively. "Daddy smells like Daddy's medicine. Daddy knows he shouldn't drive after taking his medicine."

"Give Daddy a break," Brad said.

"How was your meeting?" Juliet asked.

Brad went over to the sofa and sat down.

"Daddy wants to watch *Jeopardy!*," he said.

Watching *Jeopardy!*, which he'd been doing more or less regularly since 1984, always made Brad feel pretty smart. He knew most of the answers. Juliet had often told him he should go on the show. Brad replied, "I'm going to get on TV the legitimate way."

But now, he realized, he wasn't going to get on TV any way, ever.

He put his head in his hands. "I'm such a failure," he said. And he began to sob. "AUUUUUUGH!" he moaned.

"Oh boy," Juliet said.

She put a hand on Brad's shoulder. "Girls," she said. "Go play in your room for a while."

——

Brad wept on the couch for fifteen minutes before Juliet told him firmly, "Don't let the girls see you like this." Juliet wasn't Jewish and therefore hadn't grown up in an environment where it was considered fairly normal for men to weep at home. But she had a point. So he went into his "office," which was really just a win-dowed closet off the carport, fired up his vaporizer, and checked his e-mail, which consisted of three pieces of spam, a message from Amazon telling him he might like the new Elmore Leonard novel, a reminder that his website registration was about to expire, and a forwarded message from Alison about a script contest for "short features with a sci-fi/horror theme about Coke Zero." In other words, it was the in-box of a man without much to do. Yet still his birthday approached, as sure as the morning sun. It was time to celebrate.

Now even more stoned, Brad went inside and put on his suit, which was seven years old, but he'd worn it so infrequently that it still looked sort of new. Juliet had donned a blue velvet jacket and a flower-print skirt, as well as various earrings, bracelets, and rings that she'd bought on Etsy. She always adorned herself so beauti-fully, and with so few resources. She was a walking charm bracelet.

A neighbor lady named Linda appeared at the door, because there'd always been a neighbor lady named Linda no matter where he'd lived. Brad had met her a couple of months before when he was walking Kedzie around the block. She'd burst out of her town-home, screaming, "I admire your extremely interesting canine!" He'd started walking fast, but Linda had followed, soon telling him her entire life story, much of which seemed to involve taking mushrooms with Lawrence Ferlinghetti in the basement of City Lights Books. In recent months, she'd moved to the neighborhood because her brother had died in a motorcycle accident and now she was "seeing after his estate," otherwise known as "living in his place for free." She let Brad know that she was receiving permanent disability for an illness she refused to name. Also, she provided babysitting services for a reasonable fee.

This turned out to be fifteen dollars an hour, or, as Brad liked to call it, "the alternative minimum tax." Even thinking about going out the door without the kids cost them sixty bucks. And then Linda had just started hanging around for free. Several times Brad had come into the house to find Linda helping Juliet with her herb recipes. He'd gone out for a dog walk and had come home with an apprentice witch.

"You all have fun," Linda said as they headed out the door.

"You too," said Juliet.

"We'll just make cookies and watch YouTube," said Linda.

The older girl rolled her eyes. Brad wasn't sure why, as those were pretty much her two favorite activities.

Juliet drove them forever to a part of Los Angeles that was as unfamiliar to Brad as the nicer districts of Santiago, Chile, would have been. There were uncracked sidewalks and cheese shops and little blond children eating gelato. Cars with tinted windows and bespoke chrome bumpers glided silently down the streets as though on private tracks. The air carried just a hint of chill and just a touch of neon, one of those nights where the city seemed to promise a unique destiny to whoever dared brave its causeways. When it was all over, you were out of money.

The restaurant was called The Sideshow, not just "Sideshow," but "The," located on the ground floor of a hotel that was all white concrete on the outside and dark wood on the inside, like some kind of crazy bank that only let millionaires make deposits. The chef, who'd grown up near Coney Island but to Japanese American parents, said he'd drawn the inspiration for his place from his childhood, coining the term "raw fish Americana," which had since been repeated in every airline magazine from Dallas to Singapore. Brad knew what he was in for when he turned to his left and saw a wall-length poster, sepia-brushed to look old-timey, featuring a weight-lifting strongman with a crustacean head and the words "See the Lobster Boy."

There was no hostess stand, just an animatronic head topped with a turban. The head sat inside a glass box captioned "The Amazing Seating Machine." Earlier, Juliet had printed out a code off the Internet. She entered it into a keypad at the box's bottom. The head turned around and uttered an incantation that sounded more or less like Sanskrit to Brad. A slip of paper appeared in the slot. This contained the table number and the time of their dinner.

They went into a spare antechamber and waited in front of a red velvet curtain. Faint, tinny old-time circus music played from a speaker above their heads. Brad missed the old days in Chicago, when going out to dinner had meant a slab of meat and a martini. There were a thousand little storefronts in Thai Town where they could have eaten well for about an eighth of this money. They had nothing, but here they were acting like something. Brad was turning forty, and that was special. Dinner had to be a show. Or, in this case, The Sideshow.

At the appointed minute the curtains parted, revealing a culinary wonderland with a sawdust floor. Great bolts of pretentious red silk hung from the ceiling, swaying about in rhythmic time to accordion music that was coming from the corners of the room. All the walls were glass, showing scenes from different kitchens. Blenders whirred and cleavers thwacked. In one window, an ancient Japanese master lovingly rolled rice balls. Another showed men and women in lab coats and goggles making food with eyedroppers and test tubes. It was abattoir and laboratory all rolled into one. Aboratory. The recession had brought America to its knees, but clearly this room had been spared its ravages. Brad needed a drink.

Soon he had one too, from a bottle of wine he couldn't afford. Juliet had preordered it, and it was waiting at their table. They were deep in now. You buy the ticket, so you take the ride. A lithe woman wearing an adorable kimono and a fake beard approached.

"Welcome to The Sideshow," she said. "Have you dined with us before?"

"Not hardly," Brad said.

"Well, we don't have menus, unless you request one. Otherwise, it's the chef's favor."

First came a "mouth amusement" (as the server described it), an eight-ounce glass containing a semiviscous, deep yellow liquid topped by what looked to be a dollop of shad roe.

"What is this?" Brad asked.

"This is our fish-egg popcorn," the bearded waitress replied.

Juliet gave Brad a little smirk across the table. The server left. She raised her glass.

"Here's to fish-egg popcorn," she said, "just like Mom used to make."

Brad took a sip and then another. Suddenly, his mouth was alive with texture. The fish eggs tasted like the essence of salt. He thought he felt a taste bud actually pop.

"Oh man," he said. "This is fucking delicious."

"How did they get it to be so crunchy?" Juliet said. "It's liquid!"

"I don't know," Brad said, "but I want another."

That didn't happen, though, because next they brought him a whole white anchovy slit open at the belly. Inside was a specimen slide, topped with a light green smear.

"What am I supposed to do with this?" Brad asked.

"Lick it," said the server. "The slide itself is made of a flavorless edible substance. Then you need to bite the anchovy."

Juliet looked at him with a raised eyebrow. Brad did as he was commanded. Suddenly, his mouth was awash with the taste of the finest Caesar salad ever constructed by humans.

The rest of the meal unfolded in his mouth like a lunatic puzzle box. What appeared to be a house made of Lincoln Logs turned out to be richly spiced chicken mole topped with guacamole. A tiny little ball of potato hash exploded on his tongue on contact, filling every sense with meat, as though he'd just freebased a filet mignon with béarnaise sauce. A strand of Twizzlers contained homemade spaghetti with wild boar ragù. There were sliced meats that tasted like cheeses and cheeses that tasted like meats. Two pieces of sushi appeared, and it was definitely just sushi, but the finest sushi and strangest sushi Brad had ever tasted, as though the chef had gone fishing in some secret lake on Mars and brought his bounty home.

Brad and Juliet drank and laughed and talked, mostly about the food, as they once had done, before adulthood had caught them in its relentless treads. For once, mercifully, the girls didn't come up, and work didn't come up, and their shitty annoying house didn't come up. He didn't think about *Battlecats* once.

Two and a half hours passed this way. They brought Brad a piece of upside-down cake, literally a chocolate cake with the frosting on the bottom, which Brad thought was the one joke of the night that kind of fell flat. But this wasn't a script edit, it was dinner, and it had been completely, insanely awesome.

The check came. Brad grabbed for it.

"Uh-uh, birthday boy," Juliet said. "This is on me."

"But it's the same money regardless," Brad said.

"Still, I know how much you hate to spend money."

It was true. He had many neuroses, but most prominent among them was the idea that he simply wasn't getting his money's worth out of life. The act of buying a new pair of shoes, not that it happened that often, could send him into a spiral of self-doubt and depression. If he didn't like a restaurant meal, no matter how inexpensive, he'd save the receipt and keep it on his desk and stare at it for days, trying to figure out how to claim it as a business deduction. Now, this meal had been special, possibly the strangest and best ever, but his pernicious spendthriftery hung over him like a gassy cloud.

Juliet examined the tab. "Oh boy," she said.

"How bad is it?"

"It's bad."

"How bad?"

"Don't worry," she said. "I'll just sell some extra herbs this month."

The delight had ended. Brad's stomach sloshed full of red wine and reconstituted molecules. His guts were set on full broil. He let out a low moan. "Goddammit," he said.

His thirties had begun on a note of more than promise; he actually reached something close to *success*, at least as close to success as he'd ever hoped to come. But then it was like he'd hit one of those chutes at the top of the board that knocks you down seventy places, and it had been impossible to climb again. In actuality he hadn't risen that far and had probably only gone down about fifteen spaces, and really it was more like he was losing at Monopoly than Chutes and Ladders. Or maybe his life didn't resemble a board game at all. Regardless, as far as he could tell, forty was less than thirty.

Also, he was really drunk, more so than he'd been in months. It felt like someone had stuffed wet cotton balls up his nose. The sulfates in red wine could really do a number on your sinuses, Juliet said. His overpriced miracle-of-science dinner sloshed around in his stomach, making the final molecular transformation into shit, a perfect metaphor for what his life had become.

"We should have just eaten at In-N-Out and gone to the ArcLight," he said. "That's what we can afford."

"It's over," Juliet said. "We did it. You have to let it go."

"We need to stop pretending."

"OK. We'll stop pretending tomorrow. I promise. But tonight's your birthday dinner, so don't be such a grump."

Brad rose from the table and stumbled across the velvet baroque that was The Sideshow, parting the curtains into the antechamber and then into the hotel lobby, which was all gray and blue, minimalist art and instrumental Brazilian music playing around. The air was cool, modern, refined. By comparison, he felt hairy, bloated, and old, like a shambling rhino.

He leaned into his wife and murmured in her ear. "I'm useless, used up, and discarded."

"That's just what a girl wants to hear," said Juliet.

"Well, it's true!" he exclaimed.

The valet brought their keys. Juliet got behind the wheel. Brad stumbled into the passenger seat. He sniffed.

"Were you smoking before dinner?" Juliet asked. "It stinks."

"No, but I had some in the glove compartment."

He opened the box. There was a blown-glass pipe, seven inches long and three inches thick, inside, along with a Bic lighter. The little nub of Lemon Lift that he'd put in there for an after-dinner treat had definitely been crisped a little.

"The valet was smoking my weed," he said.

Juliet laughed.

"It's not funny," Brad said. "This stuff is expensive."

"Less expensive than that bottle of wine we had in there."

"This is bullshit!" Brad said.

"Calm down."

"I won't calm down!" he said.

Brad flung open the Prius's door and stood up, wobbly.

"Hey!" he shouted toward the valet. "Hey, man."

The valet looked up.

"Did you smoke my weed?"

"Maybe," the valet said.

Brad stepped toward him.

"Maybe? Well, maybe you should have some respect for other people's shit."

"Honey, don't," Juliet said.

"Honey, don't," said the valet mockingly.

All day, people younger than Brad had been sneering in his face. Well, he was done now with this stupid town and its pampered, entitled residents. His vengeance would begin tonight with this valet at a secret hotel that he'd never be able to afford. Brad stepped up onto the curb. His shoe turned sideways. His ankle followed. A hot shard of pain traveled up his leg.

"Fuck!" he shouted.

And he fell into the gutter.

The valets started howling and pointing. Juliet got out of the driver's seat and went over to her fallen husband.

"Are you OK?" she asked.

"It's not broken," he said.

"It's not broken," the valet whined mockingly.

Juliet looked at him with the anger of a mother bear protecting her cubs.

"Shut up, you little asshole," she said. "You're going to turn forty too someday. We'll see how you like it."

She pulled Brad up by his pits. Brad stood on his good ankle and hobbled into the car. They drove away in silence.

———

"Infinite time loop," he said in the car on the way home.

"What?" Juliet said.

"That's what I pitched to Fox today. A show about an infinite time loop."

"I'm not sure what that means."

"It's about a guy who's trapped in an infinite time loop and doesn't know how to get out."

"You mean like *Groundhog Day*?"

"No, more sci-fi. He keeps bounding around to different times of his life, and he can't get out."

"So, like *Quantum Leap*?"

"No, not at all. It's got more comedy in it than that."

"Like *Hot Tub Time Machine*?"

"No."

"Back to the Future?"

"I wish."

"So what is it like then?"

Brad sighed. "I don't know," he said. "I don't know anything."

"Just keep working on it, dear."

"They're not going to buy it. They don't buy anything."

"Well, you can't just give up."

"Why not?"

"Because, you dumbass, you have a family to support."

"My ankle hurts," Brad said.

"I bet it does," said Juliet. "I'll give you some herbs when I get home."

The way up to the house had many turns and bumps. The Prius handled it with about as much agility as an armadillo; you got them for the gas mileage, not the handling. Brad felt his dinner sloshing around in his guts like so much reconstituted mozzarella. His ankle throbbed deeply.

Limping through the front door, Brad saw Linda in the kitchen, mixing up potions.

"The girls are asleep," she said.

"How was it?" asked Juliet.

"Oh, they were very good. They ate everything I gave them, and then we played Parcheesi and watched some old episodes of *The Herculoids*. It was very enlightening."

"Sounds like it," Juliet said.

"How was dinner?" Linda asked.

Brad staggered to the kitchen sink, leaned over, and unleashed a horrific torrent of vomit.

"Oh God," he said.

"So, not good?" asked Linda.

"It was great," said Juliet. "He just had too much to eat, drink, and smoke."

"That pretty much describes the 1980s for me," Linda said.

The babysitter left. Brad sat on the couch, an herbal salve around his ankle, a mint in his mouth, and an ice pack on his head, watching an episode of *30 Rock* on the DVR.

"Look at that," he said. "Liz Lemon is a fuckup just like me, but *she* never has any trouble paying her bills, because she has a job."

"Liz Lemon is a fictional character," said Juliet.

"My life is a mess," he said.

"It's not that bad, dude. You have a beautiful wife and two girls who love you."

"That's not enough."

"It should be."

"My head hurts. I need to get stoned."

"You do not," said Juliet. "You've been stoned all evening and you will get stoned first thing tomorrow."

"So what?"

"So," she said, "what you need is *clarity*."

"And where am I going to get that?"

Juliet sat silently, lost in thought, turning her head back and forth, as though she was having a debate with herself.

"Hmm," she said. "Maybe."

"Maybe what?" Brad said.

"Hang on a second, I'm thinking."

"About what?"

"On the one hand," Juliet said to herself, moving her hands up and down as though weighing possibilities, "but on the other . . ."

"Usually a discussion involves two people," Brad pointed out.

"Shh," she said. "The witch is thinking."

The idea of a witch thinking gave Brad a little chub, so he quieted down.

Finally, after a couple of minutes, Juliet sighed and stood up. "Desperate times . . ." she said. She kissed Brad on the forehead. "I'll be back in a bit."

Brad blearily surfed back and forth between *SportsCenter* and Adult Swim. Juliet disappeared into her sunroom. Brad heard her rummaging around and some clanging and the zapping of the halogen light that she kept over some of her more sensitive crops.

"What are you doing?" he shouted back to her.

"I'm busy!" she shouted back.

"Doing what?"

"Leave me the fuck alone, dude!" she exclaimed.

Juliet was the world's sweetest person, but woe unto the person who bothered her while she was working.

About fifteen minutes passed, and then she walked through with a basket full of sprigs and sprouts and fungi, like Little Red Riding Hood in cat-eye reading glasses.

"Need some help?" Brad said.

"I've got this," she said.

"Good," he said, "because I'm having a hard time standing up."

Then she went into the kitchen, filled a huge stockpot with water, did some chopping, and boiled things. Brad watched basketball highlights. There was some clinking of glass. A half hour later, at about 1:00 a.m., Juliet returned with a little dropper bottle and a glass of water.

"What the hell have you been doing?" he said.

"Cooking," she said.

"Cooking what?"

"I want you to drink something."

"What is it?" he said. "You witch."

She kissed him on the lips.

"I barfed, you know," he said.

"I'm a witch," she said. "I've tasted worse."

She took the rubber dropper and plopped four little drops into the water glass, sloshing them around with a spoon.

"This will relax you," she said.

Brad sipped.

"Drink it all at once," she said.

He gulped. It tasted old and weedy and full of secrets.

"What did I just drink?" he said.

"Just trust me, you'll sleep great," said Juliet.

"I trust you," Brad said, "but what are you doing?"

"It's an experiment," she said. "A sort of risky one."

"Risky? How?"

"You'll be fine," she said. "I think. Now let's go to bed, old man."

Brad limped to the bathroom, changed into his stinky pajama pants, washed his face, and brushed his teeth twice. He felt pleasantly drowsy. In the mirror, his face seemed to shine out in the dingy light.

This is it, Brad, he thought. *This is all you get.*

Juliet was at the doorway of the girls' room. Cori and Claire were sleeping calmly among the stuffed unicorns and SpongeBob paraphernalia and *Amelia Bedelia* books.

"They're cute," he said.

"They're the best," said Juliet.

He wanted to give his daughters so much more than he had. This thought was usually a jumping-off point for some spectacular self-pitying on Brad's part, but not right now. Juliet's concoction was making him feel lighter and happier than he'd felt in a while.

"This stuff is great," he said. "Why haven't you given it to me before?"

"It's not something you want to take very often," she said.

Brad was so sleepy now. He could barely make it into bed. His head was on the pillow before he could even crawl between the sheets. Juliet kissed him lightly on the forehead and then on the lips. She tucked him in tight, like he was a baby.

"Thank you," he said. "I love you."

"I love you too," she said. "See you soon."

"Soon," Brad said, and then his eyes were closed.

As he drifted away, Brad could only think of three words. They repeated themselves across his consciousness like a mantra. It wasn't the mantra he wanted, but sometimes you're not able to choose.

Infinite time loop, he thought. *Infinite time loop.*

Infinite time loop.

CHICAGO
1970

Brad sensed mostly darkness. There was a little tinge of red around the edges of his perception, like the last thin corona before the sun sank away at night. Mostly, though, it was black. Not scary black, but a comfortable, warm night that would go on forever.

He also registered warmth. It was so very warm and, what was that feeling? Wet. But it wasn't wetness like after a shower or swimming. This had a thickness to it, a fluid, gelatinous quality. He was cradled like a ham in aspic. Not that he'd ever eaten a ham in aspic, but he'd seen a photograph of one in a Jacques Pépin cookbook. Maybe the fact that he was thinking in antiquated dinner-party appetizer metaphors meant that he was hungry. But he wasn't hungry, and he also wasn't full. Brad had never felt more nourished. Every cell in his body was fed, alive. His neurons snapped with pleasure.

His limbs were . . . did he have limbs? Maybe. Brad thought he could sense his fingers and toes wiggling. But mostly he just drifted, lost in a vague sea of semiconsciousness. The sounds were wonderful. He heard a kind of white noise, not like what came out of the machine that he and Juliet had bought to drown out the early-morning garbage trucks and leaf blowers and construction hammers. This was something deeper and fuller, a transmission from beyond. It fizzed and crackled, full of mysterious messages, unknowable information. In the middle of it all was a faint, deep throb, a steady pulsation. When it went, Brad sensed it not just in his ears but throughout his whole body. It was life itself, the Mind of God.

I am the star child, he thought to himself.

For eternity, it seemed, he drifted like that, with no sense of space or time. All his neuroses, his little pains, his negative and critical thoughts, his financial problems, his petty rivalries, his barely suppressed anger, his low-level weed addiction, his career failures, his bad decisions, his inability to fix his own car, his predilection toward eating salty and spicy foods when he wasn't really hungry, his eternal frustration that the Cubs were never going to win the World Series ever again, his jealousy, his half-written scripts in a drawer, his unwillingness to fully love his daughters even though they were right there in front of him, his weak and sensitive stomach disappeared into the vast liquid abyss. Brad Cohen was everything and nothing. Like Krishna, he contained multitudes.

And then it was over.

Brad felt a pressing on his head, insistent, pneumatic. It shattered his insular paradise, lasting twenty, maybe thirty seconds. But he suddenly had a sense of time; that was a bad sign.

The pressure ceased. Brad felt suction, as though he was headed up a tube. He twitched his limbs in a panic, sloshing around, and opened his mouth to cry out but tasted only fluid. Then the pressure came again, this time a little longer and a little more forcefully. The pushing was insistent, like he was a skydiver unwilling to leave the plane, or a salmon trying to escape the turbine's wrath. Brad felt himself moving downward, inevitably and forever.

But downward out of what?

He heard a little popping noise, a balloon bursting. His feet became unmoored. Now he really started to flail. He didn't want to see what was at the end.

He was being squeezed out of a tunnel by forces he couldn't control. The pressure kept coming, steady and insistent, for what felt like hours. Brad's breathing quickened; panic filled his brain.

Where am I? he thought, now fully conscious. *Where am I going? Did I remember to program the DVR?*

Though Brad didn't know it yet, the answers to those questions were, in order:

1. In the womb. Technically, in Chicago.
2. Back to the beginning.
3. You're going to have to wait a long time before you see a DVR, buddy.

Brad felt air on his feet. And then his ankles. Someone grabbed him and began to tug. *No,* he thought. *Noooooooooooo.* But it was happening. He slid down. The compression increased the farther he went, inch by inch. It felt like his shoulders were getting crushed. He couldn't breathe. Not really, anyway. Seconds passed, and he managed to get his lungs to expand and contract. They filled with fluid. He gurgled.

There was a huge tug on his backside, which was now feeling air as well, and a series of short staccato pushes on his head, which slammed him like a drum. Brad blacked out.

He woke and felt absolutely freezing. The insides of his eyelids burned bright red. He could see veins. But he still couldn't open his eyes. And his hearing wasn't much better, just a gurgling like he was at the bottom of a fish tank. That drained quickly, though, and he heard gasping and moaning, and the sound of hospital equipment, and, tinnily from above him, the distant but unmistakable sound of one of Motown's all-time greatest hits. The first three letters of the alphabet greeted him.

The Jackson 5? Brad thought to himself. *How? Why?*

If you suddenly emerged from the womb for the second time, and the first voice you recognized was Michael Jackson's, would you want to go back inside? Brad did. He still wasn't quite aware of what was going on yet, but he desperately wanted to retreat.

There was nothing wrong with the song. Far from it; despite everything, Brad knew that the Jacksons' music would endure as one of the great pop miracles of the late twentieth century, a perfect confluence of songwriting craft and youthfully innocent talent. But the problem, Brad realized, was that he *knew* that. The entire tragic arc of Michael Jackson's career flashed through his brain. Considering he still couldn't open his eyes, the fact that he was already thinking like a bad *Pitchfork* critic represented a problem.

A pair of hands held Brad by his armpits. Brad flailed insensibly. Then he felt himself being passed to another pair of hands. Brad's foot brushed against something that felt long and rubbery but also somehow *alive*. Suddenly, he knew what that was, who he was, and where he was.

Noooooo, he wanted to scream. *Don't do it!*

There was a quick snip, but it felt like someone was cutting Brad in half. He felt hot pain, sharper and more all-encompassing than anything he'd ever imagined possible. The world was cruel, unfair, and evil. A hand slapped his back.

"WAHHHHHH!" he cried. "WAHHHHHH! WAHHHHHH!"

He heard applause. The radio was now playing Sly and the Family Stone, "Thank You (Falettinme Be Mice Elf Agin)."

"WAHHHHHH!" Brad said again.

Someone said, "You've got yourself a screamer, Mrs. Cohen."

Asshole, Brad thought.

But at least the music was good.

———

Brad vaguely remembered getting put on a scale, and then some nurses giggled while they had him make a footprint, and then he got a bath in a lime-green plastic tub and was dried off by a cloth that had a crocheted duckling on it. The wall paint was light blue, the smell of cigarette smoke pervasive. Phones rang in the distance. It was 1970. Nurses were unionized and the technology was analog.

These realizations seemed awfully sophisticated to Brad. If he was really a baby, a *brand-new baby*, then how could he possibly even know his name, much less remember the commercial jingle for the brand of baby shampoo the nurses used to wash his hair? It didn't seem possible.

He moved in and out of consciousness, though he couldn't exactly figure out for how long. Time seemed to move differently when you're a newborn. But are newborns really able to perceive themselves as newborns? And are they really able to pose complex existential quandaries to themselves while in swaddling clothes? Another thing: Why could Brad remember his entire life if it hadn't happened yet? Did all humans have this level of consciousness at birth, only to have it fade away like some sort of discardable mental skin layer?

And then he thought, *Wait. I don't want to be in the '70s again. There's no Internet!*

Brad began to panic in his bassinet. But it wasn't because of the strange thoughts he'd been having. Actually, it felt like a monstrous snake was eating through his stomach lining, that a thousand cockroaches had been set loose in his gut. He screamed. A nurse rushed over to him and picked up his butt. Brad felt his sphincter unclench. His guts released a stream of gelatinous black goo, which dribbled into a cotton cloth the nurse had gotten down just in time.

"Tar's out," Brad heard the nurse say. "Let's give him to the mother."

Brad's brain relaxed. The monumental effort of his first poop had made his little baby body tired. This pattern would repeat itself throughout his life. Or it *already had* repeated itself. What was the difference? Get tense, take a shit, and feel better for a little while: the story of humanity.

When Brad next opened his eyes, he was being cradled in the loving arms of his mother, Rose Cohen. Not the mother he knew in 2010—a wiry, tracksuit-wearing busybody who spent much of her time sending angry letters about pool-water temperature to the management of the Florida active-senior complex where she lived, but the mother he *remembered* from photos and the occasional film reel—idealistic, dressed in florals, listened to Pete Seeger, lectured on social work at the university. This groovy, liberated gal of the '70s was gazing upon him beatifically, looking a little pale but still so naturally, beautifully young.

"Look at him, Donald," she said. "It's our baby! Isn't he beautiful?"

Brad swiveled his head a little. His father was wearing tweed and smoking a pipe. The tweed never went away; he was an economics professor at the University of Chicago, or at least he would become one. Now, Brad guessed, his dad was some sort of graduate assistant. It was hard for Brad to imagine Don surviving without the administrative services of a department secretary, but here he was—young, starting out. This version of the guy was dark haired, not gray or grayish as Brad remembered. Brad recalled that Don gave up the pipe in 1987 after a cancer scare. But everything else— the trim beard; the glasses; the weird, sour, distracted air—that was the same.

"Children should be neither heard nor seen," Don said.

He'd made it clear from the beginning that, while he'd never stray unacceptably far from responsibility, he was going to view parenting from a wry distance. And he held true to that for his entire life. The closest he ever came to showing Brad love was to give him his entire collection of Tom Lehrer albums. Which, honestly, was a really nice gesture, and it was all Brad had ever wanted from him. He didn't have particularly complicated feelings toward his father.

His stomach gurgled. A light discomfort settled over his brain. His hands and feet began to feel weak. Wait, he knew this feeling.

He was *hungry*.

But unlike the hunger he was used to feeling, which would pop up for five minutes and disappear immediately when he gulped down a handful of almonds, or two Cuties, or a bag of In-N-Out fries, this felt deeper, more pervasive. He was smaller, more fragile, more devoid of nutrients and good bacteria.

Then Brad realized that he didn't just feel hungry. He was *starving*. It felt like he'd never eaten before. In fact, he hadn't. He had already eaten, or was going to eat, thousands of times in the future, but that wasn't the same thing.

His body felt deeply weak, his bones ached.

He screamed.

"What's the matter with him?" Don asked, looking panicky.

"I don't know," Rose said. "Call the nurse."

Brad screamed louder. He couldn't think of anything else to do. What he really wanted to say was, "Can someone get me a *taco al pastor* or a Milky Way or something?" But his vocal cords hadn't developed yet. Even if they had, this was the era of *Rosemary's Baby*, *The Exorcist*, and *The Omen*. The boomers were really neurotic about having strange and evil children. Brad instinctively knew that the world neither needed nor wanted a talking baby.

Instead, he went "WAAAAAAAAAAH! WAAAAAAAAAAH! WAAAAAAAAAAH!," the desperate howls of a dying human.

The nurse rushed in. Brad was kicking, purplish blue.

"You've got an angry one," she said.

"Why is this happening *to me*?" Rose said, a familiar refrain to Brad's ears.

"It's not happening to you," said the nurse. "It's happening to him. I think he's hungry."

Not everything is about you, Mom, Brad thought between anguished screams.

"Have you got a latch yet?" the nurse asked.

"It's only been a couple of hours," Rose said. "I haven't tried!"

"Well, it's time."

"We're both a little tired."

"I know, dear," the nurse said. "But baby needs to eat."

So feed me, dammit, Brad thought.

But he remembered: his mother had been big into La Leche League. Back when he was born—back, well, *right now*—breast-feeding had been more than a vague political statement. It was a big deal, a major cornerstone of women's liberation, and his mother, a social worker from Hyde Park with a large library of international feminist readings, was right there at the bleeding edge.

Brad supported breast-feeding. It wouldn't have occurred to him to do anything else; it just seemed natural. Then again, Brad had never been faced with a situation quite like this, which had nothing to do about rights and had everything to do with disgusting weirdness. *His* mother was about to breast-feed *him*. No person wanted that, not even subliminally.

Oh no, Brad realized. *I have to suck on my mother's boob or I'm going to die.*

Talk about nipple confusion!

The nurse placed Brad in his mother's arms. Rose's breast popped out—a round, soft sundae cup of milky goodness. She drew the nipple toward Brad's mouth. He kicked a little, turning away, yowling with horror, but he couldn't prevent it from brushing against his lips.

"What is *wrong* with him?" Rose said. "What is wrong with *me*?"

"There's nothing wrong with either of you," the nurse said. "This is a totally normal occurrence. But if he won't take the breast, we're going to have to give him formula, at least for a while."

Rose said, "Formula goes against my convictions!"

"It does the trick," the nurse said.

Screw your convictions, lady, Brad thought. *I'm not sucking on your titty.*

But wait. Formula? This may have been 1970, but he'd already been shopping at Whole Foods for more than a decade. In the college of his future, he'd subscribe to *Utne Reader*. His wife wrote a natural health blog, or at least would. He knew all about the dangers of formula. Babies needed the good bacteria from mother's milk, or else their brains wouldn't develop properly and they wouldn't be as competitive for college scholarships. And if Brad was going to have to live his entire life all over again, which seemed increasingly likely, then he was definitely going to go to a better college this time. He didn't want to give himself any disadvantage; he was his own helicopter parent. Drinking his mother's breast milk would be the best first step. All the books said so.

I'll do it, he thought. *But I won't enjoy it.*

He swatted at his mother's breast.

"I think he's trying to tell us something," Rose said.

Brad gave another swat.

"Looks like he's ready," said the nurse.

Don Cohen puffed on his pipe, watching quietly and half-interested, as though this were a televised Dick Cavett interview program rather than the primal drama of life.

The breast drew closer to Brad, areola beckoning like an open four-lane highway. Brad was headed toward Mount Nipple. He tilted his head and tried to think everything he could that didn't involve the disgusting reality of his mother's nipple sliding between his puckered lips.

A squirt of warm, delicious, infinitely nourishing mother's milk shot into Brad's mouth. He recoiled. But then it went down into his stomach and he instantly felt better. He pulled from the teat again. The milk tasted even sweeter. The act itself may have been disgusting, but the food was incredible, of the highest-possible quality. Brad was the ultimate locavore. He felt himself surging with energy and secret microbial vitamins.

Brad sucked and sucked, and then he sucked some more. Then he sucked himself to sleep and then pooped in his pants while he slept, and when he woke up he was eating, and then he fell asleep again, an infinite cycle of nectar and rest, with occasional interstices of getting his butt daubed by cool powder.

A man could ask for no more.

THE '70s

At first, Brad existed in a total state of existential panic, which you're allowed to do when you're an infant, the only time of life when constant, terrified screaming is considered even remotely acceptable. But then his throat started to hurt from the endless caterwaul. So he descended into a kind of mopey resignation.

What choice did he have? He couldn't exactly petition the government to reinsert him into his proper timeline. All he knew was that his wife had given him something to drink, and he'd taken it, and then he'd woken up in the womb.

You witch, he thought. *I'm going to find you and then . . .*

But according to this timeline, Juliet hadn't been born yet. Even if she had, he didn't know her phone number. And even if he did, he wasn't physically capable of dialing it. Also, he had no proof that she'd done this to him. Or that anyone had. So he was pretty well stuck. If there were any metaphysical lessons to be learned from his strange situation, he didn't even remotely know what they were. Whatever wormhole he'd been sucked through didn't offer up answers very easily.

Regardless, he didn't enjoy being a baby again. He was always tired, absolutely exhausted, just from the very effort of breathing air. When he *was* awake, he was either wetting himself or totally starving. The breast-feeding never got less weird, especially several times a day. And when finally, mercifully, the weaning process began, his parents started feeding him flavorless mashed peas and disgustingly sweet apricot jam while their own meals of broiled meats and steamed vegetables made his stomach moan. It was '70s food—flavorless and unimaginative—but at least it was *food*.

His first Passover was the worst, as his nana—who died, or was going to die, when Brad was five—came over and made the most extraordinary-smelling seder menu that Brad had ever experienced: a genuine old-country feast of boiled chicken, homemade gefilte fish, and latkes that would stop a cop's heart. The house brimmed with chopped liver. Brad had to eat breast milk and liquefied carrots.

Also, he couldn't walk. Admittedly, there was something appealing about getting gently pushed around in a stroller in the sunshine. Everyone could benefit from that treatment once in a while. But Brad's *primary activity* was getting walked around the same pond at the same time every day and being shown the same three mangy urban ducks. It got boring.

He was constantly shitting and pissing himself and could do absolutely nothing about that. Since Brad was physically unable to walk or talk—though perfectly capable of reading that vintage *Esquire* magazine that sat on the couch tantalizingly out of his reach—he could neither get to a toilet nor really indicate that he wanted to use one. By the time his parents responded to Brad's screaming, it was always too late! A great lake of warm, disgusting, humiliating brown mush had spread across his ass.

One night it all came to a perfect head when Brad's parents took him, in his fairly relaxing bouncy baby carrier, to a Chinese chophouse, a real one, only a fifteen-minute drive from their house.

They put him on a table, and Brad had to watch as an extraordinary array of lacquered ducks, Chinese broccoli in oyster sauce, dumplings, and noodles was paraded before him.

The treasured delicacies of the Orient!

His mother put a drop of soy sauce on her finger. Brad sucked at it like a starving vampire.

Please, he thought. *Just one meatball. One dumpling. One taste of real human food.*

At that moment, Brad's bowels rumbled. He could feel the train a-coming. A-rolling round the bend.

A tremendous geyser of digested mincemeat and green-bean puree erupted, covering his butt like ash on the slopes of Pompeii. *"Brrrrrattttt!"*

"*Someone* had to go!" Brad's father announced.

Brad's face turned red with embarrassment. But he was *not* going to scream. Instead, he was going to sit there indignantly in his poopy pants, the smell spreading like an evil mist.

"He needs to be changed," Don said.

Rose looked distraught. "Our food just got here," she said.

"There's nothing I can do," Don said, "because there's nowhere for me to change the baby in the men's room."

"Oh, so there's room to smoke, but you can't wipe your son's ass?"

Great, Brad thought. *Now my parents are bickering about me.*

"My hands are tied, dear," said Don, holding up his hands, which were quite obviously not tied.

Rose huffily picked Brad up and carried him into the ladies' room, which was small and cold, concrete, just a sink and a toilet, a mop and bucket. It was tight in there. Brad's mother had to maneuver him out of his jumper. Because she was an expert, she managed to avoid making a big mess of the room, handling the situation like the fixer she was.

However, she didn't avoid accidentally dropping Brad in the toilet.

For many years, the story of "I dropped Brad in the toilet when he was a baby" would be a hit at dinner and bar mitzvah parties, a beloved family anecdote. In the past, Brad had always laughed along with his family. But that was because he couldn't *remember* it. "Dropped in the toilet" was a hilarious abstraction. But now the past was the future, and he was doomed to remember it all over again.

"It was such a small bathroom," Rose said later in bed as she and Don were roaring with laughter at Brad's expense. "*Everything* was over the toilet. His arms just slipped, and there he was, sitting plop down in the toilet bowl!"

Brad, who at that point was still sleeping in their bedroom, heard every word.

"He's our little flushable baby," Don said.

I am so much more than that, Brad thought.

Five minutes later, it got worse. Brad's parents started having sex. It was the first time since Brad had been born. He closed his eyes tightly but could hear every grunt and shuffle and snort and moan. No child should have to know that his mother is a screamer or that his father's orgasm noise sounds like the bray of a terrified gnu. But Brad was cursed with that knowledge now forever.

Then, mercifully, finally, Don was snoring. Rose smoked and read a Joan Didion essay in the *New York Review of Books*. All the great magazine articles of the early '70s, and Brad was missing them so that he could get dropped into toilets and listen to his parents fuck.

This, Brad thought, *is the worst day of my life.*

Either of my lives.

And then he shit himself again.

For a long time, it seemed, he was Baby Brad and nothing more. Then one morning he felt power in his legs. He lurched toward Don's easy chair, grabbed on with his hands, and pulled himself up with tremendous effort.

Now what? he thought.

But Brad knew. He hadn't walked for a year, but he'd walked for four decades before that, all over Chicago and New York and a bunch of other cities too. One time he'd walked to the top of the third-highest peak in Rocky Mountain National Park. He'd run cross-country in high school. He could do it again.

Brad, who'd watched far more cheesily inspirational Lifestyle Network movies than he'd like to admit, felt an imaginary orchestra swell in his head. He made a little gurgling noise to make sure his parents were watching. They were. They were *always* watching because he was the best show in town. He was their baby.

And then Brad let go of the chair.

He stood there wobbling, but like his Weebles, he did not fall down. His shaky little dough knees hesitated, but then Brad felt them straighten. They snapped into place like buttons. He moved one forward. It stuck. Then another and another. Suddenly, he was moving.

"Don, look," Rose said. "He's walking!"

Don took his pipe out. "So he is," Don said. "Look at that."

The inspirational music in Brad's head swelled. It was all sweetness and violins. Rose held out her arms. "Come here, baby," she said. "Walk to your mama!"

Brad smiled, mostly toothless. "WAAAA-HAAAAAAA!" he cried.

He staggered forward, mobile, alive, adorable, and free. He was no longer a human houseplant, 100 percent dependent. If he could do this, then soon he could feed himself, and very, very soon he could walk to the toilet and sit on it. He didn't care if it was a year and a half ahead of his development schedule. This was Brad's independence day, the first of many.

He ran into his mother's arms. She enveloped him, as she was wont to do.

"Such a good boy," she said. "I'm very, very proud of you!"

Brad gurgled. Don patted Brad's head.

"You know what?" Rose said. "This calls for brownies."

Brad squealed. His mother's brownies were the best!

"Sounds like somebody's hungry," Don said.

Brad was so hungry. Especially for brownies.

For the next few months, he ran shirtless and gloriously free in the Chicago midyear sun, shrieking across the playground with joyful abandon, tearing around Grant Park during a jazz festival, down the sidewalk, across the apartment and then upstairs, running and leaping and tumbling down the Michigan Dunes. He gloried in his incredible body, which seemed to be padded with eight layers of foam, so unlike the sore and brittle middle-aged bag of blood and bones that Brad had left behind. The winter of his discontent had turned to glorious summer.

His parents started letting him watch television, and things got even better. He was from 2010 and therefore used to being continually entertained. But he also remembered TV, good old-fashioned four-channel TV. He longed for it. Then, one morning Rose needed to get some work done, and she turned on the PBS block of *Sesame Street* and *Mister Rogers' Neighborhood*.

The screen was tiny, almost pointillist in its lack of clarity. Most of the time, the picture seemed blurred and fuzzy. You had to turn knobs to fix the picture. But Brad didn't care. He luxuriated in a warmly flickering cathode bath.

It was TV! At last!

Brad didn't need *Sesame Street* as preschool. He was already more or less not racist, and he knew how to count to ten. Give him a sheet of paper and he could even do simple algebra. Not only did he know the alphabet, he knew the Russian *and* Hebrew alphabets. But TV still accomplished its pacifying magic. He sat gurgling, humming along to old Cookie Monster songs he remembered, enjoying it when Ruth Buzzi showed up, and wryly observing that Bert and Ernie really did seem like a weird middle-aged postsex married gay couple. He legitimately laughed, flapping his arms because he could. His parents found that really cute.

The TV went in spurts at the Cohen house, based on whether his parents were getting along. If the marriage were on sound footing, they'd often spend the evening reading, talking and smoking, sometimes with other couples. There were dinner parties and Dylan albums on the hi-fi. But when things dipped domestically, usually during those dim periods where Don was having passive-aggressive affairs with grad students, the TV started coming on at night as well.

It was mostly early '70s stuff that Brad had previously only seen in reruns. *The Bob Newhart Show* and *The Mary Tyler Moore Show* had intelligent humans who understood comic timing at the helm. But almost all the other shows were unwatchably moronic, especially seen through the prism of a failed twenty-first-century TV writer. Brad watched *Laugh-In*, President Nixon turning to the camera and saying, "Sock it to me?," cringing at how weak the material actually was, though he did like Jo Anne Worley.

Watching television was strange for Brad, and it just got stranger every day. He knew what was going to happen, maybe not in specific episodes, but in general. WJJM would shut down, Mary would be the last one out of the room, and Lou Grant would resurface a few years later without a laugh track as a California newspaper editor. The jarring appearance of Cousin Oliver meant that *The Brady Bunch* was about to cross over into oblivion. From now on, Brad would know the ending of more or less every movie and TV show, definitely every Super Bowl. He'd also know the ending of every famous person.

One night NBC was rerunning Elvis's *'68 Comeback Special.*
Brad had never seen it before. It was exhilarating to watch the King
at the height of his gyrating, spangled, long-haired, gospel-tinged
middle period, before the fall.

This is entertainment, Brad thought.

"Elvis!" he exclaimed.

"What was that?" asked Rose.

Brad had been able to talk for a while now. But he'd been waiting to spring some sort of iconic first word on his parents. A simple "da-da" wouldn't do.

"I think he said, 'Elvis,'" Don said.

"Elvis!" Brad said again.

"Our baby is talking!" Rose said, "And his first word is 'Elvis.'"

But Brad took it a little too far.

"He's going to die on the toilet," Brad said.

"*What?*" said Don.

"He just said that Elvis is going to die on the toilet," Rose said.

"I want him to say it again," Don said.

"Uhhh," Brad said. "Elvis?"

"No, son," said Don, "say *exactly* what you said before."

Brad's parents looked at the strange beast they had created, the
boy who, before his second birthday, had predicted the exact manner of Elvis's death. Their gazes held a mixture of fear and wonder.
It was more than he'd ever inspired in them the first time around.

"How do you *know*?" Don said.

It was only 1971. People didn't want to know the truth about
their King. And if Brad came out and said to them, "I've lived this
exact life before and I know everything that's going to happen
until 2010," they would have him hospitalized forever. Then, once
his predictions started to come true, he'd end up in a government
research institute, simultaneously probed, harassed, and shunned,
like some sort of third-tier X-Man. That wasn't what Brad wanted.

Right there he made a conscious decision to project a vague illusion of normality until it was acceptable to do otherwise.

He wiggled his arms, touched his nose, and pointed at Don. "Da-da!" he said. "Yaaaaay!"

It worked pretty well. Brad's parents got a lot of subsequent mileage out of the fact that Brad's first word had been "Elvis." They always omitted the "He's going to die on the toilet" comment, though, because, let's face it, that positioned their son badly. They preferred to paint Brad as a kind of quirky, bell-bottomed pop savant, not a sinister doom prophet.

In reality he was neither. He was a man in a boy's body forced to live through the 1970s for a second time. The decay, the disillusionment, the *malaise*: Brad could feel it bloom like a cloud over Three Mile Island. Vietnam would go horribly wrong; Nixon would get caught and flee in disgrace. There would be gas lines and an Islamic revolution with a hostage crisis that would top the decade like a rotten cherry. Brad could see it all coming. It was like he was living in the past, the present, and the future all at once. He tried to ignore it like so much background static, but it was always there, always on, and always calling.

His life felt like a repeat, dished out in thirty-minute, commercial-soaked increments. Single-box TV served him a constant mental diet of all-knowing nostalgia, one scoop of vanilla, when what Brad really wanted was a twelve-flavor banana split with whipped cream, cherries, nuts, sprinkles, and six different toppings, including pineapple. *Scooby-Doo* and *Super Friends* were fine once in a while if they came on Boomerang and you were high and you could click away whenever you wanted. But there was no Boomerang. Or Netflix. Or Internet. Or anything. There was barely even HBO. Brad couldn't click away. And he was, regrettably, never high.

Most of the time, Brad kept it to himself, but he'd occasionally drop a smart bomb just to fuck with his parents. A simple viewing of *The Love Boat* could turn into an existential crisis.

"Hah," Brad said. "Gopher."

"This show is the worst," said Don, who nonetheless tuned in for every single episode that guest-starred Charo.

"Gopher," Brad said, "is going to be a reactionary Midwest congressman someday."

Don looked at Brad with a little fear, which he always did when Brad was entering soothsayer mode.

"Oh, come on," Don said.

"It's true," Brad said. "He's going to be in Congress, and so is Steve Largent of the Seattle Seahawks."

"You're just making this up."

"And Sonny Bono," Brad said, a statement that caused Rose to spit out her wine.

O. J. Simpson, wife murderer. Michael Jackson, child molester. Kermit the Frog on the cover of *Vanity Fair*. Abba on Broadway. Don and Rose would be plagued by weird aha moments their entire lives, continually tripped up by their son, the snarky prophet.

One Saturday afternoon, a Ronald Reagan western was "Movie of the Week." Don turned it on. Brad moaned. The Gipper appeared on horseback.

"That man's going to be president," Brad said.

Don just laughed. But he'd lived with this strange boy for a while. He knew that, when it came to really important matters, what Brad predicted always came true.

A couple years later, America elected Reagan in a landslide. Don called a psychiatrist.

For himself.

THE '80s

The years passed, and the world caught up with Brad. He could relax a little into his second incarnation. The world had less to fear from an eleven-year-old who talked like a grown-up than it did from a three-year-old who did. Don got tenure and stopped screwing around, Rose got into natural health, and Brad got into comic books. Family life normalized.

In May 1981, Brad's parents took him to see *The Empire Strikes Back* on opening night. Brad had begged them, even though it would be technically the sixtieth time he'd seen the movie. He was still looking forward to seeing *Empire* on the big screen again after all these years. But he was also operating on a metalevel that no one else on earth could understand. Brad *really* wanted to see the faces of the other kids when Darth Vader made the big reveal. He wanted to remember wonder, what it was like when the world was young, before spoilers, before Jar Jar Binks ruined it for all of us.

"We could go see it at the Ford City Mall," Don said.

"On *Cicero*?" said Brad. "That place is horrible. The screens are so small."

"Look who's Gene Siskel all of a sudden," Rose said.

"We have to go downtown to see it on a big screen," said Brad.

Don thumbed through the *Sun-Times*, what he called a "workingman's newspaper" even though he was no workingman himself.

"It's playing at the Esquire," he said. "We can go to the Berghoff afterward."

That sounded like a good night. Brad and his parents took the bus over to Thirty-Fifth Street, transferred to the El, and sat on the train as it dimly chugged down to the Chicago Avenue stop, where, underground, an old man played "Sweet Home Chicago" on a beat-up Stratocaster with a portable amp barely bigger than a desktop radio. Brad had spent most of his life in Chicago once, so it was kind of weird to go back and do it all again, especially now that Chicago had mysteriously reverted from the yuppiefying boomtown of the '90s back to the gritty Chicago of *The Blues Brothers*, when you could actually still see Junior Wells on Maxwell Street. It was like watching urban renewal simultaneously in forward and reverse. He didn't even remember what it was like to live there when a Daley wasn't in charge. Now he knew. It was awesome. Also, it smelled like pee.

Brad tipped the blues guitarist thirty-five cents, his Junior Mints money.

"What'd you do that for?" Don asked on the stairs up.

"I like the blues," Brad said. "I can relate."

Don and Rose thought that was very funny.

"What have you got to feel the blues about?" Rose said.

If they only knew.

They walked east toward the lake. The Esquire, a grand, 1,400-seat movie palace from the Golden Age, was definitely not at its height in 1981. Plitt Theatres, that not-so-great name in cinema history, had taken it over, letting the stuffing come out of the balcony seats. The carpet had frayed, the bathroom sinks leaked, the walls were oily, and the upper balcony rows reeked of sex and booze. Brad knew the Esquire's future. It would be multiplexed into banality in 1988 and then close for good in 2006, though with the big orange-and-yellow neon sign still out front to remind people of a time when the Gold Coast was sort of interesting.

They turned onto Oak Street. Brad saw the neon and the awning. The marquee read:

20th CENTURY FOX PRESENTS
THE EMPIRE STRIKES BACK
DIRECTED BY IRVIN KERSHNER

Now that was something Brad could feel freshly excited and nostalgic about at the same time. It was so amazing, he wanted to use his phone to tweet a picture. But there were no phones, at least not ones that could take pictures, and there was no Twitter. There was only memory and a big salted tub of half-rancid popcorn and a watery Sprite that could float a barge and a box of Junior Mints that would sit like a flaming brick in Brad's stomach for two days.

They sat through a preview of *Raiders of the Lost Ark*, which was *also* coming out that summer to blow everyone's mind. Everyone stared at the screen raptly, no matter how old they were. They had no phones. They weren't particularly distractible. Movies went on and on, and they'd sit for hours, just happy to be entertained. Brad looked around him and saw 1,250 people staring in innocent wonder at the blockbuster world. The beautiful fools, they had no idea what was coming. George Lucas would betray them all.

Don *must* have enjoyed the movie, because he always walked or took the bus and never sprung for a cab. But on this day, after the movie was over, they took a cab down State Street to the Berghoff, where Don had reserved a table. Brad loaded up on sauerkraut and the biggest damn plate of knockwurst he'd ever seen. Don ate pig's knuckle. Rose mopily stirred a bowl of gelatinous stew. She never liked what she ordered.

"I can't believe that he's Luke Skywalker's father," she said.

"An actual plot twist," Don said. "Who'd have thunk it?"

"I knew," Brad said. "I've known forever."

His parents looked at him and sighed.

"Of course you have," said Rose.

———

Brad lived mostly in his mind, apart from other kids. He did well in school, definitely top 10 percent (except in math, where he still veered toward the middle), but not so well that he'd draw suspicion to himself. He could bang out a five-paragraph paper in twenty minutes. He had a lot of free time and didn't do much.

"Why don't you ever play with other children, Brad?" Rose Cohen asked him.

"Because they're boring," Brad said.

"You wouldn't know unless you talked to them."

"I've talked to them," Brad said. "I know."

But sometimes Brad invited other kids over to play Atari, because it was always better to play video games with kids. He had the 2600, the 5200, and the Intellivision, and the ColecoVision. All the visions. Whenever a new system came along, he boxed up the old one, with all the games, in boxes labeled, "Precious Childhood Artifacts. Do Not Discard." He knew that people would pay a lot someday for antiquated gaming systems in decent working order.

Brad was also an arcade warlock in a way he'd never been the first time around. He kept an eye out for new consoles. When Centipede and Galaga, games on which he already had a head start, appeared, he went at them with a fistful of quarters. He concentrated on those, because he knew they had staying power. Maybe he should have been learning French. But level thirty-two on Joust was also a laudable goal.

Brad knew that, someday soon, nerds would rule the world, and he knew exactly what they valued. He became a collector, like in *Guardians of the Galaxy*, which he also collected. But unlike the first time around, when the comics had come in the mail and he'd torn into them like a hungry dog, this time every issue went straight into the plastic case, to be unearthed twenty-plus years later, along with a tremendously valuable cache of twenty thousand other comics and *Star Wars* figures and Nolan Ryan commemorative no-hitter Topps cards.

He didn't read any of them. The Frank Miller comic-book shot-in-the-arm was still years away. Jack Kirby was rolling in his grave. Except that Brad didn't think he was dead yet.

Hey, he thought. *Maybe I could meet Jack Kirby.*

So he wrote Jack Kirby a letter.

"Dear Mr. Kirby," it went. "My name is Brad Cohen. I am eleven years old, and I live in Chicago, Illinois. In my opinion, you are the greatest comic-book artist of all time . . ."

Jack Kirby never wrote him back, but it got Brad into a new hobby. He sent lots of fan mail because he could and because he knew whose autographs would be worth something in years to come. Mostly, he asked people who he knew weren't going to get out of the early '80s alive. It was cynical. He couldn't save them, but he could cash in on them at auction. Andy Warhol and John Lennon never fulfilled his requests.

Most people didn't, but occasionally the mail would yield a nugget. John Cleese sent a signature on a piece of stationery that had a dead parrot at the top, and Mel Brooks sent an autographed photo. He got a handwritten note from Johnny Cash that went, "Dear Brad: Thanks so much for your kind letter. Sorry I haven't written back sooner. It's been a dark period for me. But I'm glad that young people today are still liking my music. Good luck with everything and stay happy. Best, Johnny Cash."

That one got framed. For the rest of his second life, Brad would display it on the wall of his office. Whenever anyone important dropped in, he'd turn it into a talking point. It became a pillar of

Brad's reputation, which probably isn't what the Man in Black had intended.

His body, thin and hairless, was growing like some sort of sharp-jointed alien emerging from a pod. Every day revealed a new angle or a fresh rib. Brad looked at himself in the mirror for hours. Thirty years forward, he knew this body would be hairy and bloated, with strange warts where they really should not exist.

Now he stood at the brink of boyhood's end. He'd gone from being the old man in *Death in Venice* to Tadzio. It was a reprieve for sure. He'd been looking forward to this phase for a long time.

Boy, did he miss sex. The first time through, even at the supreme nadir of Brad's misery, when the world had seemed broken and hopeless, he and Juliet had still been going at it three times a week, sometimes only twice if the kids were sick and keeping them up at night. He had not been a sexually frustrated man.

Yet here he was, a virgin anew.

Sex was the best thing in the world. And he was pretty *good* at it, especially compared to most twelve-year-olds. He had several decades of experience, which had given him a couple of good moves and a reasonably decent sense of timing. He longed to get back in the game.

But how? Certainly not with anyone he knew. Brad's biological age was twelve, but his chronological age was fifty-two. The thought of kissing a girl made Brad feel like a pedophile. His wife, the only sexual partner that he could fully remember anymore, the woman who may or may not have put him in this situation in the future, or the past, or whenever, was at this point a nine-year-old girl in suburban Cleveland. He couldn't exactly call her up and proposition her unless he wanted to get sent to a juvenile psych ward for the rest of the 1980s.

To make things worse, Brad had the interest but no actual sex drive. Puberty still hadn't struck; his body contained about as much testosterone as a Vampire Weekend tribute band. His hairless dingle hung between his legs, as lame as Tiny Tim on Christmas Day, a urinating pseudopod.

Every day for several hours, Brad went into his bedroom, pulled down his Jockeys, and stared wistfully downward at his minischlong. He knew it could achieve so much more. But no amount of concentration on mental images of Heather Locklear in her *T. J. Hooker* police uniform seemed to be able to will it into existence.

He locked his bedroom door.

Come on, big guy, he said to himself. *I know you're in there. Warrior, come out to plaaaa-ay!*

He thwapped away at his appendage like a cat playing with a nip-filled ball, but the winning formula eluded him.

God, what if it's just not going to happen in this lifetime? he thought desperately. Maybe that was the point. Maybe whoever was making him repeat his life over again was trying to teach him that sexual desire was bad. Maybe he was doomed to live forever as a biological oddity, a eunuch, a hairless Ken doll.

Or maybe not.

He kept trying. He thought hard. It's not like he had anything better to do. And there was so much great wanking material in those days. Lynda Carter as *Wonder Woman*. Any of the Charlie's Angels, even Tanya Roberts. Chris Evert grunting in her tennis dress. Erin Gray. The deliberately welcoming thighs of Miss Ginger Lynn Allen. Kathleen Turner in *Body Heat*. Hell, even Miss Piggy in the right light . . .

Brad felt a rumble in the Bronx, a stirring below.

Come on, he murmured to himself. *Come on!*

He felt an inching up his belly, a worm after a good rain.

His stamen was swelling, engorging with blood. But the battle hadn't been won yet. It could always retreat. Brad closed his eyes and concentrated, not touching anything, letting his body find itself. A baby bird needed to leave the nest on its own. He thought harder. His body felt tingly and alive.

Then he opened his eyes and looked down. His dick had returned. It was there, twitching, just below his belly button. The fact that this boner had been induced, at last, by thinking about the Muppets didn't make it any less his.

Hello, old friend, Brad said.

He gave it the greeting it deserved. Cue the masturbation montage.

It went on for months. This wasn't your ordinary sexual awakening, no innocent amateur hour. Brad raised masturbation to the status of divine art. He had *technique*. He was a master. A master bater. He knew how to pace, to cup his balls, and to gently massage his perineum. He was the only thirteen-year-old on earth with a makeshift butt plug fashioned from a desktop eraser. There was more than a decade of pent-up grown-man lust in Brad's body, and he didn't care how loudly he grunted while sliding his hips up and down the inside of his closet door. Brad would have rolled around by himself on a bearskin rug in front of a fire if he could, whanging the whole time. He was writing the *Kama Sutra* of schlong wringing.

Brad's masturbation career reached its glorious apex one Sunday afternoon, as Don and Rose went downtown to hear a talk by the Dalai Lama. Brad remembered that event from the first time around. Their seats would be obstructed-view, back row. And then Don would have a painful but not serious sinus attack and end up at the emergency room, spending six hours watching *Murder, She Wrote*. The family would return home six hours later, exhausted but with an eight-ounce squeeze bottle of high-powered prescription nasal spray. That was plenty of time for a jerkfest.

As soon as Don and Rose locked the front door, Brad dashed to the bedroom with a Price Club–sized bottle of hand lotion and two rolls of toilet paper. He was so excited that he squirted almost the moment he touched himself. But it didn't matter. Five minutes later, he was ready again. He had so much to give!

After the second time, which took a little longer but not much, Brad followed a hunch. He went into his dad's study—Don was a U of C professor, and by then they had an apartment that was half a city block long, with a view of the lake, no less—and followed his nose to Don's cigar cabinet. He opened it and immediately saw a half-smoked joint there among the Cubans.

Oh, sweet, magical weed! Brad thought. *I have missed you so.*

Brad took the joint as his birthright. He hadn't been high in nearly thirteen years. He went into his bedroom, opened a window, and inhaled. It tasted dank and bitter. God knew how old this joint was, or where the weed had been grown. But Brad didn't care. It was stressful to live your life over again, and he was high at last.

He came eight times. Then nine. He was an autoerotic menace, Onan the Barbarian, the emperor of hand cream. It seemed to go on forever.

His parents walked into the living room. The Dalai Lama had ended the talk early in this timeline, and Don's sinuses were fine. Brad was sprawled on the sofa. It smelled like the upstairs rooms of Studio 54 in there.

"Son of a bitch!" said Don.

"Crap," said Brad.

"Oh my!" said Rose.

"I can explain," Brad said.

"No need to explain, I get it," said Don.

"What do you mean, you *get* it?" Rose said.

They started bickering.

Brad lost his boner. But at least he knew where to find it now.

Brad Cohen became a bar mitzvah—again—on Saturday, March 5, 1983, at Congregation Beth Israel on the South Side of Chicago. This wasn't some new, flashy, suburban temple celebrating forty-plus years of successful assimilation. No, this was the place where Saul Bellow had been bar mitzvahed. The sanctuary dated back to 1923, ancient by American standards, and the congregation's history dipped all the way back to the 1860s—*actually* ancient—long before large numbers of Jews sought asylum on American shores.

Also, somewhere along the way Beth Israel had gone reform. Men and women could sit together. Sunday school became more "cultural" and less about memorizing liturgy with a grumpy old Pole traumatized by his treatment at the hands of the Cossacks. By the time Brad arrived, the music and lyrics of Debbie Friedman had drowned out the tired, droning men, replacing it with a more laid-back, heartfelt "Kumbaya" vibe. They were all Free to Be Jew and Me. The congregation had a long-haired rabbi who played the organ in his overalls at Beth Israel's summer camp in the Dells. Yom Kippur services included a slideshow of nature scenes accompanied by a recording of "Morning Has Broken." Sung by *Cat Stevens*, for God's sake. The enemy of the Jews!

The study process was easier the second time through, though just as unenjoyable. Brad didn't start from Aleph-Bet ground zero. He was stringing together vowel sounds and reading simple sentences by the time he was nine, knocking out basic prayers by age ten, and fully locked in on his Torah portion well before his big day. Brad actually had time to dig deep on the haftarah, just because he could. He memorized a double portion, singing using the traditional Askenazic melody.

One day after lessons, the slack-jawed cantor went up to Don and Rose and said, "Your son is the finest bar mitzvah student that

I've seen in forty years. I have never seen such a thorough work ethic. He will succeed at anything he tries."

Don and Rose were really surprised, but then they always were by their son. Brad rarely tested as a genius. Most of the assessments placed him at above-average, but hardly extraordinary, intelligence. But when it came to application, he was the best. He had a deep internal drive to succeed, powered by some mysterious infinite source.

They didn't have to know that Brad was so far ahead because he had a forty-year head start, and that his "drive" was actually highly calculated and somewhat cynical laziness. His strategy now was: take the same classes again, put in just a little extra effort, and rise to the top like delectable cream.

It was the era of Alex P. Keaton. People valued a certain kind of raw starched-shirt intellectual ambition. This time around, Brad was going to be a kid who fit in with the grown-ups.

Of course, that meant there weren't a lot of kids in the temple on Brad's special day. Don had three sisters, and Rose had a brother and a sister each, so there were cousins, lots of them, plus a half-dozen guys who Brad had played video games with. This helped lower the average age under sixty. But it was still an old shul filled mostly with old shul-goers.

There Brad stood, in his blue yarmulke and flowing tallith, the arc glowing golden behind him, sacred letters inscribed on sacred wood, a gateway to the mythical old man in the sky who harshly watches over us all. The rabbi turned to the ark and chanted on his heels as the congregation. Then he opened the ark. The light of God didn't come pouring out. No one's face melted. Instead, there sat the Torah, rescued from Poland like all good Torahs, resplendent in gilded brocade and white cloth. Out it came, with a loud *sh'ma*. The rabbi walked up and down the aisles, singing:

Blessed is the Lord who gave us the Torah

Blessed is the Lord who gave us the Torah
Blessed is the Lord who gave us the Torah
Torah, Torah, To-rah!

Brad followed behind, trying his best to look as though he was into it. All of Brad's parents' friends were beaming at him. He was smiling back. He was going to give them a show. Brad wanted to impress the *alta kockers*. He had a bowl haircut and braces so thick they could have borne the weight of the Southern Pacific line. In other words, an archetypal bar mitzvah boy. This is what they'd all come to see. Today he was a Nice Young Man.

Brad knocked out his Torah portion, no problem. He wailed through that haftarah like a confident champ. Then came time for his sermon. In his first incarnation, Brad had lazed off the task completely, forcing Rose to slap something together for him at the last minute, which she did reluctantly, cobbling together a few hundred words, half of which seemingly were "friends" and "family" and "tradition," culminating with the corny line: "And now the words that you've all been waiting to hear—the buffet is open!" Brad delivered it without much enthusiasm.

This time, though, it was a thousand words of pure prophecy from a prodigal child who, at age two, had accurately predicted that Elvis would die on the toilet. Brad would hide no longer. It was time to reveal his powers to the world.

"Ladies and gentlemen," he said, looking outward, "beloved friends and family . . ." He turned his gaze left on the bimah, where sat the temple's two rabbis: Lipstein, the boomer hippie, and Sherman, older, more hidebound.

"Rabbis," Brad said, "and congregants, we live in a time of immense conflict and great social change."

"Oh, brother," Brad could hear Sherman murmur behind him. But Brad pressed forward.

"My Torah portion today was taken from Exodus, the most profound literary expression of the desire of a people to be free. Today, we're free to congregate as Jews because of that desire, and because of the sacrifices made by millions of our ancestors. And we should be equally grateful to the founders of America, who waged war so we could have the freedom to congregate under a religious banner as we see fit."

At this point, Brad had cobbled together a reasonably decent paragraph from an average newspaper editorial, sentiments in a can that he could easily deliver at Boys State without offending anybody. But then he pivoted.

"But we have to remember that, even as we today celebrate our freedom, there are millions of people all over the world who don't have that luxury. The black people of South Africa live under a cruel system of apartheid as severe, violent, and unjust as our former Jim Crow laws."

Rabbi Sherman, a Reagan voter, moved in his seat uneasily, as did quite a few of Brad's relatives.

Brad continued: "Central Americans find themselves daily brutalized by corrupt dictatorships, many of them propped up and funded by the US government for vague and cynical reasons. And in our own country, gay and lesbian people find themselves denied a whole raft of basic civil rights, including the freedom to marry and to adopt children."

That brought about a little gasp. This was 1983, after all, and the Gay Plague had just started to descend over America. He intended to be an advocate long before it became fashionable. Even now, he was right, as he would continue to be, about everything. And he knew it. So he continued as the crowd looked on, stunned by this very strange speech.

"Indeed," he said, "our very notion of the word 'freedom' is extremely malleable. We're free to drink ourselves under the table, as long as we don't drive. But if you get caught with a joint in your pocket, you could go to jail for years, particularly if you're black or Hispanic. How far are we willing to extend our freedoms? Where is the Exodus for people convicted of innocent, consensual crimes?"

Other than the fact that it came out of the mouth of a bar mitzvah boy, that didn't raise a lot of controversy. Not in the liberal lakefront district that was soon to help elect Chicago's first black mayor. But Brad was saving his money shot, the one that would make the bimah shake. He uncorked.

"We, as Jews, are just as complicit. While I believe that the state of Israel has every right to exist and to thrive, I also don't believe that it should be used as a cudgel to keep down the Palestinian people, who have just as much a historical claim to the land as we do."

"Lies!" Brad heard from the crowd. He looked up. His mother's cousin Charlie had risen to shake a finger. There were boos and murmurs. Brad's would have been a controversial opinion in 2009. But in 1983, at the height of Yasser Arafat's career, it was heresy.

"Search your heart," Brad said. "You'll know it to be true."

Over in the rabbi corner, Sherman whispered to Lipstein, "Who does this little shit think he is?"

"I happen to agree with that little shit," Lipstein whispered back.

"Maybe I should tell that to the board when it's time for you to take the senior rabbi job away from me," Sherman said.

"Go ahead and do that, you fucking dinosaur," Lipstein said.

"Don't you mouth off to me, boychick!" Sherman said, loud enough for the whole congregation to hear.

While the rabbis bickeringly tugged at each other's tallith, the rest of the congregation murmured, some more loudly than others. But Brad didn't want the congregation to leave thinking that Rose and Don had raised an enemy of Zionism. He had much more complex goals.

"On the other hand," he said, "let's not glamorize the situation in the Middle East. Islamic radicalism in Iran is a real threat to freedom, especially to ordinary Iranians, who are fleeing to America to find a better and more prosperous life. Also, if we're not careful, propping up Islamic radical fighters in Afghanistan to fight the Soviet Union will lead to more trouble and despair than we could possibly imagine."

Brad looked out at the crowd. No one had any idea what he was talking about. The Taliban didn't exist yet, and neither did Al Qaeda. But they would soon.

Brad had stumbled into a method that would give him the moral high ground in every possible writing situation. There were differences between this timeline and his first timeline, but they were so subtle and minor that they didn't seem to matter. So, he figured, he might as well give the *illusion* that he was helping to push things forward, that he was in some small way an actor in that history. Along the way, he'd stir up people. It was a winning formula for success.

Brad thanked the crowd once again for coming. Then he said, "And now the words that you've all been waiting to hear—the buffet is open!"

After the service, Brad's uncle Alan approached.

"Interesting speech," Alan said. "A little thin, though, more than a little didactic, and inconsistently argued."

It's always hard to impress family.

———

One afternoon a couple of years later, Brad was sitting at home watching *Battlecats*. Old habits died hard. He'd snuck a couple of puffs off one of Don's joints.

It was the episode where the Clawmaster, the rogue druid who was constantly battling Prince Catspian for control of the Battle

Kingdom, pretended to ally himself with the Dog Army, only to change sides at the last second, preserving peace, allying himself with King Tom Tabby, making himself appear like the savior of the Battlecats while secretly positioning his laser cannon to destroy the capital. It was actually a surprisingly successful political allegory of the times, one that Brad and the writing staff had never been able to recapture in the reboot that had destroyed his career in Hollywood. Now as the first run reappeared in the culture, Brad sat through every new episode. He needed to be familiar in case he had to work for *Battlecats* again.

Don came into the room. "What are you watching this crap for?" he said.

"I dunno," Brad said.

"You've got better things to do," said Don.

Don didn't say stuff like this often. He didn't need to. Brad usually *was* doing better things. But he clung to *Battlecats*, the last vestige of his former life. Why, though? This second incarnation seemed to be doing just fine. He had no real reason to watch other than to glimpse the occasional cheesecake shot of Panther Lady.

"You're totally right, Dad," Brad said, and he turned the TV to *Wall Street Week*. It was time for Brad to pursue a higher, older ambition. Why cling to failure when you had the power to fabricate success?

Cats would battle no more in Brad's life. The *New Century* awaited him.

This time he'd stay a lot longer than two months.

THE '90s

The *New Century* had been the leading magazine of ideas and opinion in American life since its inception in 1890. This was, admittedly, a bit before the actual new century. But the magazine's founder, a somewhat overly well-read industrialist named Horace Gladstone, considered himself a forward-thinking person. In the founding editorial, he wrote, "It is my intention to encourage America to adopt new technology, to keep the tax base moderate, to be mighty with the sword but diligent with the olive branch, and to promote freedom and opportunity for all people no matter the circumstances of their birth." Gladstone split the middle of the road of opinion exactly down the middle, a winning formula that ensured the *New Century*'s editors would always be a hot date in the capital's salons.

One morning in April 1990, Brad Cohen walked into the *New Century*'s offices, on Twenty-First Street in Washington, DC, with the intention of joining their number. He carried with him all the confidence that one-and-a-half lifetimes could allow. For young men of a certain ethnic background, with a certain amount of ambition, and a taste for spending their working hours reading dreary old *Congressional Record* summaries, looking for a juicy policy tidbit, the *New Century* was the absolute best possible place to land. Brad shared the ethnicity and ambition but not the proclivity toward research. He didn't need documents, because he already knew everything that was going to happen—at least everything that mattered. That gave him quite an edge.

He leaned up against the receptionist's desk. The receptionist was thin and small and ten years shy of elderly. She wore a sleeveless blouse and glasses so thick they could have doubled as car headlights. Her desk was about as tidy as the floor of the Chicago Board Options Exchange at closing bell. She was on the phone.

"I'm sorry," she said. "Mr. Rosenstein is in a conference right now."

She was talking about *Gary* Rosenstein, the legendary biker professor of Harvard Yard and also the longtime arts and letters correspondent of the *New Century*. Gary Rosenstein had slept with two of Norman Mailer's wives and possibly with Norman Mailer himself, and had somehow pulled off the trick of hanging out at both Andy Warhol's Factory and Nixon's White House. He was the only man in American who had Lou Reed *and* Henry Kissinger in his Rolodex. One time he'd broken Leonard Michaels's nose at a party on a bet.

Gary Rosenstein had spoken not one word to Brad in Brad's previous tenure at the magazine, which had, technically, taken place a year in the future, but it was also twenty years in the past. Brad wasn't going to get ignored again. Or maybe he was. Rosenstein ignored everyone. Either way, he was determined to make a better show of things this time.

"May I take a message?" the receptionist asked.

A pause.

"OK," she said. "How do you spell that?" And then, as she wrote, she said, "*U-p-d-i-k-e.*"

Another pause.

"OK then, Mr. Updick," she said. "I'll have Gary call you as soon as he can."

Brad suppressed a laugh. Actually, it was more like a scream.

A door burst open. There stood Gary Rosenstein, his delicious mane of hair terribly disheveled, first three buttons of his collar open.

"Was that call for me?" he said. "I was expecting one."

"Yes," she said. "It was a Mr. Updick from Massachusetts."

Gary Rosenstein sighed. "That's Up*dike*, Susan," he said. "John Updike. The famous writer."

"Well, he called you."

Rosenstein rolled his eyes and went back into his office. Ten seconds later, the door opened again. CNN's chief congressional correspondent walked out, patting down her hair, and left the room without looking at Brad or anyone else. That was a typical Rosenstein lunch hour.

Finally, Susan, who Brad knew from past or future experience was everyone's receptionist, acknowledged Brad's presence.

She looked up at him. "How can I help you, young man?" she said.

"I'm here for my interview," Brad said.

He gave her his name, and she looked down at her desk.

"Yes, you're on the schedule," she said. "Just wait here and they'll come get you."

"Thanks," Brad said, and then, winking, added, "I call him Mr. Updick too."

"Who's Mr. Updick?" she said.

———

The *New Century*'s current owner was Jacob Jaffe, a Yale professor of economics and also the second son of one of New England's largest shipping families. He'd bought the magazine for pennies on the dollar in 1968 after the *Washington Post* had taken a brief but disastrous milquetoast stab at it, and immediately brought it back to political relevance by tacking its politics hard right, publishing witty screeds against the counterculture and women's liberation, and even, in one dark hour, a cover essay titled "Is School Busing Really Necessary?" Of course it was, but Jacob Jaffe wasn't necessarily in the game to be right.

In 1972, just to stay in the conversation, Jaffe ordered the magazine to bank left. He rode Nixon hard. Admittedly, so did everyone else, but the *New Century* dug its spurs in as deep as anyone until that horse rode out of town. They published attacks on the CIA after the Allende assassination, had a correspondent in the Killing Fields of Cambodia before it was fashionable, and published an early piece on Harvey Milk and the new politics of gay liberation. Ralph Nader wrote a cover story about corporate propaganda, and Noam Chomsky submitted a dense tract called "The Banality of American Fascism."

As you can imagine, that got boring pretty fast. That era's writers had since gone on to bemoan the decline of organized labor elsewhere. Recent years had seen Jaffe broach the middle. Starting in 1981, he employed a raft of senior editors, all of them hosts or panelists on at least one national TV show, whose opinions split exactly down the middle between "Reagan is an idiot" and "Reagan is a god." This made for editorial meetings where everyone screamed at one another across the table all the time like undergrads in the cafeteria. It worked on TV, but it made managing the staff a pain in the ass. By 1990, the Reagan enchantment had begun to dissipate. Jaffe once again sensed a shift in the political winds. He was looking for a way to enter another phase. His way found him.

Brad Cohen entered Jacob Jaffe's office. It was a large office, wood paneled and professorial. Volumes of philosophy and history and journalism lined the walls, from Herodotus to Susan

Faludi, with not much fiction or poetry mixed in. The arts were Rosenstein's department. Jaffe liked the serious stuff that moved the world forward.

He was reading the *New York Times* and the *Wall Street Journal* simultaneously, skipping back and forth between articles on the same topic, trying to read between the lines to figure out the *real* story. This was a hobby of his, an intellectual exercise like doing the crossword. Brad cleared his throat. Jaffe didn't look up.

"Mr. Jaffe," he said.

"Yes?" Jaffe said without looking up.

"I'm Brad Cohen. I'm here to interview for the junior editor position."

Jaffe looked up. "I'm sure you are," he said.

They all looked the same to Jaffe, these eager young Jews with their big ideas and their starched collars. He knew them because he had once been one of them. Every year he handed out three junior editorships to the country's most promising young future pundits, thereby filling the ranks of Washington journalism with his disciples and greatly reducing his risk of being attacked in a rival publication. It had worked for a long time.

"I've been reading your clips," Jaffe said to Brad's surprise. "I liked that piece you wrote in the campus magazine comparing the autobiographies of Benjamin Franklin and Donald Trump. Very clever."

"Thanks," said Brad. "I like that one too."

"My one question is: Why waste any column inches at all on a nothing like Donald Trump? *Spy* chewed him up years ago."

"He's not a nothing," Brad said. "An idiot maybe, but a consequential one. In fact, I think the Donald will be a player in American business and entertainment for the rest of his life. He could easily host a TV show. Even run for president."

"Donald Trump will never be president."

"Of course not. But he could be a candidate."

Jaffe pointed at Brad. "You," he said, "are crazy."

He picked Brad's résumé off the desk.

"Let's see," he said. "Two-time high school journalist of the year. National Merit Scholar. Graduated from the University of Chicago, Phi Beta Kappa, with a double degree in political science and economics. Finished in two and a half years."

Jaffe paused and lowered his glasses halfway down his nose, unimpressed. He saw kids with credentials like that all the time. The junior editor gigs were tough to get.

"What?" he said. "No Rhodes Scholarship?"

"I'm not really a jock," Brad said.

"Hah," Jaffe said. "Me either. A little racquetball and running maybe."

"Besides, I'm too selfish to be a Rhodes Scholar."

"Some of the most selfish people I've ever known have been Rhodes Scholars," Jaffe said.

This was Brad's in.

"You mean like our future president?" Brad said.

"And who might that be?" said Jaffe. "Donald Trump is no Rhodes Scholar."

"No," Brad said. "But Bill Clinton is."

"Bill Clinton?" said Jaffe.

"Yes."

"The governor of Arkansas?"

"Yes."

"Hang on a second."

Jaffe pressed a button on his phone. "Susan," he said. "Could you tell Gary I want to see him."

A minute later, Gary Rosenstein came through the door.

"You rang, *mein Führer*," he said.

"Yeah. This is Brad. He's applying to be a junior editor."

"A *Jew*nior editor," said Gary Rosenstein with a studied sneer.

"Brad, tell Gary what you just told me."

"Bill Clinton is going to be the next president of the United States," Brad said.

Jaffe and Rosenstein had a good laugh with that one. Brad sat stoically.

"May I make my point?" he said after the yuks had subsided.

"By all means," Jaffe said, daubing his eyes.

"He's young, he's handsome, and he's about as aw-shucks as they come. And even though he has the most elite education imaginable, no politician fakes the common touch better. He's the smartest man in any room, and he's politically ruthless. When it comes to free trade and economics, he's basically a Republican, but he also doesn't play these bullshit trickle-down games, and he's tough where he has to be on foreign policy. And let's not forget his wife, who has a legitimate chance to someday be our first female president."

Again, Jaffe and Rosenstein laughed. Again, Brad regarded them stonily.

"You can mock if you want," he said, "but the Clintons are the ultimate modern power couple. They are going to seize control of this country and remake it in their boomer-yuppie image."

"You're serious about this, aren't you?" Jaffe said.

"I may or may not be serious," Brad said, "but I'm definitely right. Give me this job. Assign me a cover story on Bill Clinton. I'll prove it to you."

"Junior editors don't usually get cover stories. Mostly, they make copies and do research for the senior editors."

"I'll do all of that," Brad said. "But also give me the Clinton story. I'll stay on that beat for two years until he's elected."

"The junior editor position only pays two hundred dollars a week," Jaffe said. "Which is why the positions are usually summer internships."

"Money's not a problem," Brad said. "I invested all my bar mitzvah gifts in Apple stock."

Jaffe and Rosenstein gave each other a look. They wanted to pivot the magazine again. This kid clearly had a vision. If he was wrong, they could always dump him. Jaffe said, "How about we make you a senior editor instead?"

━━

The appointment of an unknown twenty-year-old—and one without an Ivy League degree, no less—to their ranks had the rest of the *New Century*'s editors in a frenzy. They'd never been on this side of an editorial sea change. The churning waters were making them a little sick.

They sat in the *New Century*'s conference room, awaiting the arrival of their new colleague.

"What were they thinking?" said Arnie Kaufman, a staunch libertarian with modest predilections toward technology and corporate largesse.

"You've got to serve time in the bullpen," said Mark Dubinsky.

The bullpen was where the junior editors sat, alongside the fax machine and the LexisNexis console. There were four of them, hip to hip, back to back, constantly on the phone checking facts, awash in a sea of research printouts and tear sheets while also desperately trying to find the angle that would secure them a slot in a private office. Each senior editor had one of those rooms with a door, ringing the bullpen like luxury boxes. Once your name went on the door, it rarely came off unless life took you elsewhere. Becoming a *New Century* senior editor was no one's life ambition, but it *was* concrete in which that ambition could rest.

"Everyone pays their dues," said Mark Dubinsky's twin sister, Tessa. He was a Republican and she was a Democrat. Both of them were nerdy-cute, in their early thirties. They were in discussion to set up a he-said, she-said debate show on CNN to follow *Crossfire.*

Also in the room were George Brook, a terrifyingly hawkish refugee from a pro-Reagan think tank, and Eddie McCord, the youngest and most recently hired of the group. Brook was always wrong about every major issue of the day. He stated his opinions in muscular and witty prose that almost made it acceptable that he had a side gig taking corporate speaking fees. Jaffe kept him around because he brought in a certain wealthy audience.

McCord was the cultured one, under consideration in the highly unlikely event that Gary Rosenstein would abdicate his valuable throne at the top of Mount Critic. He made his first splash with the publication of a cover essay, "The Bisexual American," the first such piece to appear in any magazine with even a pretense of mainstreamness. Since 1987, he'd kept the magazine on the people's side when it came to the AIDS crisis and the banning of gangsta rap, and on the establishment's side when it came to the encroachment of political correctness into college curriculums. He was Jaffe's version of the youth movement, a bulwark against the magazine seeming too square and wonky. The fact that he was a bit of a dull pedant, and also in his midthirties, didn't seem to hurt his rising reputation as a voice of the new generation.

There they sat with four other men: a science guy, a defense specialist, an economist, and a thinly disguised political operative, all of whom were forty-three, all bespectacled, and all Harvard graduates. All told, they represented the *New Century*'s hive mind. The prospect of a new arrival threatened everything.

Brad Cohen entered the room with Jaffe and Rosenstein. He had the body of a twenty-year-old but the experience of a sixty-year-old. This made him far more dangerous than any of the senior editors could imagine. They may have been smart, but he'd actually lived through the '90s before. Being able to predict the future with nearly 100 percent accuracy was a great gift in this line of work.

Jaffe took his place at the head of the table, and Rosenstein sat at the other end, like parents at seder. Brad sat next to Jaffe.

"OK, everyone," Jaffe said. "Item one, the only item that really matters. This is your new senior editor, Brad Cohen."

"His name was created by a random-Jewish-name generator," Rosenstein said.

Everyone laughed, including Brad, because it was basically true.

"Hold on a second, Jacob," said Mark Dubinsky, because they all called Jaffe by his first name; the *New Century* was a family until it wasn't. "Why does he get promoted like this? Tessa and I served our time in the pits, and the rest of us started on the bottom somewhere."

There was a murmur of agreement. Brad was clearly an interloper, an undeserving. He wasn't even old enough to drink! But Brad had thought through this situation very carefully. He knew who these people were and more or less where they were going; a couple of them, he couldn't quite remember, but it was nowhere important. He'd been studying them for two lifetimes, and he was ready to take them down, mostly by waiting them out.

Other than McCord, who would prove remarkably resilient, and Gary Rosenstein, who was probably a vampire, the rest of them had a career shelf life of five to twelve years. The Dubinskys would retreat to university life after disastrously backing Al Gore in the recount fight. Jacob Jaffe himself would suffer a fatal heart attack while skiing in Vermont in 2004. If Brad just gave them what they wanted now, he'd outlast them all.

"Brad, maybe you want to address that," Jaffe said.

"Of course," Brad said. "Look, I'm not here to be a threat to you all. I wasn't even looking for a senior editor job. Jacob just offered me one, whether I deserve it or not, and it would be foolish of me to turn it down. But I'm not going to take one of the private offices. I'm going to sit in the bullpen with the other juniors. You all can use me as you see fit—research, phone calls, whatever. I won't get your lunch or your coffee—that's below my pay grade—but in any other way, I'm yours."

"So why is he a senior editor then?" asked Kaufman, addressing Jaffe directly, as though Brad were incapable of answering for himself.

"Brad's got a story he's going to be working on," Jaffe said. "His beat exclusively."

"And what's that?"

"It has to do with the next president."

"Does he know something we don't?" asked George Brook with a huge guffaw.

"He thinks he does," Jaffe said.

"Well, tell us then, kid," Brook said, turning to Brad Cohen.

"The next president of the United States will be Bill Clinton," Brad said.

The conference room exploded with laughter.

"The governor of Arkansas?" said Brooks.

"That guy is a *hillbilly*," Kaufman said.

"He's a hillbilly who went to Yale Law School," said Brad. "And a lot more Americans can relate to a guy from Arkansas than can relate to a guy like you."

That shut Kaufman up for a second.

"Look," Brad said. "I don't mean to insult anyone. I know it sounds crazy, but I'm telling you, I've been crunching on this story for a year, and I just have a feeling about Clinton."

Brad went ahead and listed all the reasons, all the anecdotal evidence he had. America was ready for a Democrat who was simultaneously pro- and antibusiness, for and against the workingman, and more or less with it culturally. It was the great hour of boomer ascendancy, Brad said. The *New Century* could ride that wagon straight to the White House.

The room was quiet.

"I can see it," said Lenny Wasserman, squinting carefully at Brad.

Wasserman, if history repeated itself—and, in Brad's experience, it always did—would go on to become one of Clinton's primary White House fixers. So it made sense that he was inclined to believe. Everyone else seemed to regard Brad with something between confusion and admiration. Since when did a twenty-year-old walk into the office and proclaim the next president?

"There are a lot of negatives on Clinton too," said Brooks. "Or so I hear."

Brad wasn't doing this to be a Clinton booster, though he had voted for the Big Dog in 1992 and '96 the first time around and would almost certainly do so again. All he cared about was predicting the future accurately, and an accurate future would include a Clinton White House besieged by scandal. He'd be on top of all of every morsel well before it dropped.

"I'm not going to sugarcoat," Brad said. "There are some sketchy real-estate dealings, and he has a problem with the ladies. Like a beyond-JFK problem."

That seemed to get everyone's attention. Brad gave them whatever details he remembered, leaving out the semen-stained blue dress worn by Monica Lewinsky, who at that moment was enjoying being a high school student in Los Angeles, blissfully unaware of her future role as the president's mistress and a failed purse designer. But Brad did say, "If Clinton wins, the possibility of shenanigans in the Oval Office goes up by about a thousand percent." Why not?

By the end of the meeting, Brad was one of them, before he'd ever taken up his perch in the bullpen, a junior editor who was really senior, or a senior editor who ate lunch with the juniors. Regardless, he was on the team now.

"Cohen," said Brooks.

"Brooks," said Cohen.

"I need some research on Saddam Hussein. Ever heard of him?"

Brad reached into his shoulder bag, shuffled through it, and pulled out a thick manila folder full of clips and policy papers with key passages highlighted. He knew what was coming, and he was ready for all contingencies.

"Hopefully this will get you started," Brad said.

Brooks flicked through the folder. It had everything he needed, and more. He puckered his lips in appreciation.

This kid was good.

———

For two years, Brad worked the pen, putting in fourteen-hour days, interrupted only by power jogs on the National Mall, never abdicating except for a quick trip home during Passover. This was the era of the Gulf War. The *New Century* got very busy and serious of purpose during wartime.

The first time through, Brad had experienced the Gulf War as follows: it was on TV. Then one night, this painter he was trying to score with took him to a protest in Grant Park. They got stoned and had ended up getting chased down the street by baton-wielding men on horseback. Then they took the bus to Wicker Park, drank a lot of whiskey, and screwed on a mattress in an unheated loft.

Now he was faxing documents to the Brookings Institution. The previous life may have been a lot cooler, but this time Brad had a long-term strategy. The seniors needed Brad to research, to wonk, to place calls to Saudi Arabia. He did everything they asked, plus extra, working uncredited, unsung. One night a couple of weeks before the whole calamity wrapped up, he tapped out an editorial called "Finish Hussein Now, or Face the Consequences Later." Brad went to Jaffe's office and showed it to him. Jaffe devoured it in one bite, like a truffle. He had never seen a piece of writing so nerdily prescient, full of unassailable logic and pertinent facts.

"We have to run this as the lead," he said.

"Great," Brad said, "but do it without a byline. Or just credit the Editors."

"Are you sure?"

"I don't care if people know I wrote it. I just want to make sure that it gets said."

Of course, everyone who mattered knew that Brad had written it. When it became the most-discussed piece of the week, Jaffe let him go on CNN to talk, the first of what would become a seemingly infinite number of appearances. After that he started asking for and receiving occasional flights for reporting trips in Arkansas. Clinton built momentum. So did Brad.

On March 17, 1992, the night Clinton knocked out Paul Tsongas by winning the Illinois and Michigan primaries, Brad was in Chicago at the big room in the Palmer House Hilton. He milled around, looking for quotes. Someone tapped him on the shoulder. Brad turned around. It was Rahm Emanuel, who, Brad knew, would one day be a congressman and a chief adviser to Barack Obama, though Brad didn't know he'd also become mayor of Chicago. That lay beyond the scope of Brad's crystal ball.

"Brad Cohen?" Rahm Emanuel said.

"Yes?"

"Big Dog wants to see you."

"As long as it's on the record," Brad said.

"He's the presumptive Democratic nominee, you dickless fuckstick," said Rahm Emanuel. "He'll be whatever he wants to be."

"Fair enough," said Brad.

They walked through the crowd, snaking behind the stage and down a marbled hall. Emanuel opened up two enormous oak doors. There sat Bill Clinton, chatting loosely with a bunch of suits, some of whom Brad recognized from his past/future, some of whom seemed unfamiliar.

"This our guy?" Clinton said. "He looks barely old enough to vote."

"I wish," Brad said. "First time I cast my ballot, I voted for Michael Dukakis."

That got a laugh.

"So listen, I was wondering," said the Big Dog. "We've all been reading your pieces in the *New Century*. You've gotten everything right. Not every detail, but everything that matters. But none of us have ever talked to you except for the gal who faxes out the press releases. Who are your sources?"

"I don't have any sources."

"Don't be coy. This is confidential."

"I'm not being coy," Brad said. "Guess I'm just really good at reading the tea leaves."

"That you are," Clinton said, and then sat in his chair, looking thoughtful. In a different era or even a different setting, he would have sucked on a cigar. "Why don't you come work for me?" he asked.

"Sir?"

"If I win this thing—"

"*When* you win this thing," Brad corrected.

"Right, when I win this thing, I'm going to need the best people. I get the sense that you might be one of those people."

How wrong you are, Brad thought.

"Thank you, sir," he said.

"How would you like to come work for me in the White House?" asked Clinton.

"In what capacity?" Brad said.

"An advisory one," said Clinton.

"What kind of advice could I give you?"

"I don't care how young you are. I need people who can read the tea leaves."

"That's very flattering, Governor Clinton," Brad said. "But—"

"I don't recommend you turn me down," Clinton said. "The benefits will be enormous."

"Undoubtedly," said Brad. "But I'm not interested in being Rasputin. I prefer to maintain my independence. Can I recommend my colleague Lenny Wasserman instead?"

Clinton sighed. "Lenny's already been on the payroll for a year," he said.

"Oh," said Brad.

"Are you sure you want to keep your little magazine job?" Clinton asked.

Brad sensed they were trying to hire him to shut him up. He was going to get put in charge of Global Youth Strategies or some such bullshit. And if he stayed around, an extended turn in the Clinton White House also probably meant an interrogation for the Starr Report. Brad was happy to spend years reporting and commenting on the Contract with America and Whitewater, but he didn't want to have to play fixer with them, even in a third-hand way.

Brad extended a hand. Clinton shook it.

"Best of luck to you, Mr. President," he said.

"So I'm going to win," the Big Dog said, smiling.

Brad held up his index and middle fingers.

"Two times," he said.

"I'll hold you to that if you're wrong."

"I won't be wrong."

They showed Brad out. Brad exhaled, and then he jumped around a little bit. It had worked! He'd gone one-on-one with the man who, ten months from this moment, would be the president, and he'd played hard. He'd even turned down a job offer from the White House. His second time through life, Brad Cohen was nobody's patsy, nobody's weakling.

"You are the best," he sang while jumping around. "The best the best the best!"

From behind him, he heard a drawl.

"Well, you certainly have a high opinion of yourself."

Brad looked around. There stood an attractive woman, sandy-blonde hair overteased and oversprayed but with expensive materials. She wore a power suit with big shoulder pads. Her eyes glinted with wit. Brad blushed.

"I was just joking," he said.

"Sure you were, Brad Cohen," she said. "You know you're the best the best the best."

"You know who I am?" he said.

"We all know you," she said.

"What do you mean?"

She extended a hand. "I'm Karen Stafford," she said. "From Little Rock. I do fund-raising for the governor. And other candidates sometimes."

Brad took it. Her grip lingered a beat, and she let it go slowly.

"You have pretty eyes," she said, and winked. Brad felt he could almost feel the heat and crackle. These Arkansas people were shameless.

"Come with me," she said. "Let's watch history."

They moved out of the gallery and into the crowd. There was a roar. Clinton took the stage.

"The people of Illinois and Michigan sure know how to celebrate St. Patrick's Day," he said.

Hillary was onstage too, clapping as the Big Dog spoke. He was done in a minute, and it was mostly celebratory platitudes. Then confetti dropped, flooding the room with colored paper. The AV system boomed "Lean on Me," the dreadful 1992 Club Nouveau version, Clinton's first theme song before the machine settled on Fleetwood Mac.

All around Brad people were hugging and kissing and celebrating the birth of a glorious new America. He was in the middle of the party wearing a fairly expensive tie.

Karen Stafford tugged at his arm.

"This is a big night," she said. "I want to celebrate."

"So celebrate," he said.

"I want to celebrate with you."

An hour later they were in Karen's hotel room at the Hilton, the first of many hotel rooms they'd share over the course of that summer and then from time to time in Washington after that. It would be a gloriously superficial coupling, neither of them really paying attention to the other while both of them chugged along on separate career fast tracks. In that sense, it was like all of Brad's other relationships the second time around. But this one pushed venality to the maximum.

Karen popped a bottle of champagne. Brad guzzled it. Karen slid her hand to his crotch and undid his zipper.

"Show it to me," she said. "Show me your big Jew pundit dick."

Now *this*, Brad thought, was different.

———

Two days after Clinton's inauguration, Jacob Jaffe announced he was stepping down from the helm of the *New Century*. The logical candidate to replace Jaffe was Gary Rosenstein, whom he asked but who he knew would decline, because the increased responsibility would get in the way of his lifestyle. Jaffe had other ideas. He and Gary called Eddie McCord and Brad Cohen into his office. Brad sensed what was coming. Eddie clearly had no idea.

"So, you are my two best candidates," Jaffe said. "And I trust that the magazine would be in good hands no matter which of you took it over."

McCord interrupted. "I just wanted to say, Jacob, that if you ever want to come back to work for whatever reason, I'd be glad to step aside at any minute."

"That won't be necessary," Jaffe said.

"Just an offer," said McCord.

"Because I'm giving the job to Brad."

Brad smiled just a little. That was his strategy in this lifetime: no whining and no bragging, just pure confidence. Besides, this hardly came as a surprise to him.

McCord, on the other hand, was very surprised, and he sputtered madly. "*What?*" he said. "But he's twenty-two years old! And he's never worked anywhere else."

"He also correctly predicted the results of the presidential election two years out," Jaffe said. "And was right that the Republicans would seize Congress. He's been right about everything."

"Dumb luck," said Brad. False modesty was another one of the tenets in his self-faith.

"Maybe," said Jaffe, "but I'm interested to see where Brad takes us in these '90s."

"Well, fuck that!" McCord said.

"Sorry you feel that way."

"I earned this job."

"You did," said Jaffe. "But you didn't get it."

"So I quit," said McCord.

A week later Eddie McCord took a columnist job at *Newsweek*, the first in a series of high-profile gigs that he'd trade in every two or three years, like a leased car, for better-paying gigs at other publications.

Jaffe kept his corner office. He said he was now "editor emeritus" and would advise Brad on how to steer the editorial. Often that advice would come via phone from Connecticut, where Jaffe had a house. He claimed to be writing books but seemed to spend a lot of time skiing in Europe.

Brad was in control of the *New Century*.

Under his watch the *New Century* was on the money when it came to Rwanda and Bosnia and covered NAFTA from every side of the aisle. Brad wrote pinpoint editorials on why Hillary's health plan would fail and why Newt Gingrich's seemingly doomed Republican revolution would also blossom into something more sinister down the way. He predicted the inflating and the bursting of the first tech bubble, getting every single market fluctuation exactly right. There were early calls for gay civil rights and an extended early essay on "Larry David and the Comedy of Nothingness." That last one didn't really stick the landing; cultural criticism wasn't Brad's specialty, and he still had weird, jealous feelings about TV from the first time around. But other than that one obvious weak spot, he knew exactly what to say, and when. The magazine thrived.

So did Brad. There were always parties, and they always ran late, or there were rock shows to catch at the Black Cat. He caught bands at the best phases of their careers, or veteran solo artists who he not only knew were going to die, but knew *exactly* when they were going to die.

Where was Juliet in all this? He didn't know, and, he was almost embarrassed to admit, he didn't really care. At this point he was too far down a different path, dating too many different people, to bring her into the mix. He was a different person now, completely. He had different friends, in a different city, but he was having even more fun in Washington, DC, than he had in Chicago the first time around. His social status was so much higher. He actually got invited to parties. Any domestic capital that he'd built up in his previous go-round had been discarded like low-value start-up stock options.

Yes, Brad missed his family, but who needed them? He was on a magical cruise through prosperous times. And he was really enjoying his twentysomething's body too. He could drink more than two beers without falling asleep, could run a few miles without too much trouble, could drop a tab of E at a Saturday night rave and only need Sunday to recover, instead of the entire next week.

But after Clinton took office the second time, Brad began to feel sad and uneasy, even as the rest of the world partied on. Everyone else acted like the sunny skies would last forever. Brad knew what was coming. The next ten years offered nothing but conflict and anger and death. He could smell the mold long before anyone else.

Brad's writing started taking on a gloomy quality. It was still prescient but not in a way that people wanted to read. He did a profile of George W. Bush. Going down to Austin and interviewing Bush cronies just made him depressed. As the 2000 election neared, Brad warned that the vote would be close, "Maybe even contentious in a way that we haven't seen in a century or more," but he took no pleasure in this prediction.

Brad was no longer enjoying his little prophecy game. He didn't want to be part of the cleverocracy anymore. One weekend, after polishing off a futurist editorial headlined "Y2K Is Nothing Compared to What Comes After," he took the train up to Connecticut, where Jacob Jaffe always had a guest bed made up for his greatest protégé.

Jaffe picked him up at the New Haven station. They drove back to the house, had dinner with Jacob's family, and afterward retreated to the study to spark a fatty and drink brandy. It was the civilized way to live.

Outside, the air was appropriately stormy.

"I'm a fraud," Brad said to Jaffe.

It was the first time he'd admitted anything even remotely honest to anyone in thirty years. It felt good.

"I know that," Jaffe said.

"You *do*?" Brad said.

"Of course. I'm a fraud too. A total fake."

"But this is different. I—"

"Look, Brad, we all foolishly believe our opinions, our ideas, our low-rent sophistry is going to influence the course of human events."

"I kind of hoped *mine* would," Brad said. Actually, he didn't care at first, but now that things were about to go sour in the world, he did.

Jaffe puffed off his stogie and sipped at his brandy. His brand of sophistry had paid for a lot of refinement. He was a successful fraud.

"No one can control what happens in the world," he said. "History marches forward no matter where we stand on the chess grid. There are systems in place that we, as individuals, can't even begin to influence. All we can do is be as intelligent and discerning as we can and try to land on the right side of history. And you're the best at that I've ever seen."

Brad sighed. This sort of dime-store neoliberalism worked in the '90s as an effective tonic to the death anxiousness of aging boomers, but it meant nothing. It was easy to talk about the End of History when history was going good. Meanwhile, Brad knew, Hurricane Katrina was only five years away.

"Things are going to get bad," Brad said.

"Of course they are," said Jaffe. "They always do."

"No," Brad said. "Really bad."

"Sure," Jaffe said.

Jaffe had been a campus radical during Vietnam, but the intervening years made him soft. His conception of "bad" didn't include the most horrific terrorist attack in human history, catastrophic wars, government-sanctioned torture, an almost complete melt-down of the global financial system, and a massive, ice-cap-melting weather apocalypse. All of that was coming, and soon. The next decade would be a grim blockbuster played out in real time.

"I can't work at the *New Century* anymore," Brad said.

Jaffe didn't look surprised. "I figured as much," he said.

"I'm sorry. You were good to me."

"No need to apologize," Jaffe said. "You had a good run at a hard job, and I'm forever grateful for your help."

He extended a hand. Brad shook it gratefully. Everything about his career may have been a lie, but Jacob Jaffe was still more of a mentor to him than he'd had in either life.

"So what are you going to do, young man?" he asked.

Brad had to warn the world. But the *New Century*, he knew, was so last century. Only one place would matter as the apocalypse unfurled. He would join the media revolution before the media even knew that it was revolting.

"I'm gonna be a blogger," he said.

THE '00s

It was almost impossible for Brad to make a bad investment. He would never have to worry about money, which was good, because he sure wasn't making any as a freelancer. All through the spring of 2001 and into the summer, Brad sat in his underwear in his Adams Morgan, DC, town house, living on takeout, banging out thousand-word warnings about potential terrorist attacks. It was a tough sled. People were online and reading, but Facebook and Twitter were still years away. Also, his writing had a kind of sweaty urgency, a shrillness that people didn't necessarily want to hear.

Brad couldn't help himself. September 11 was coming, but no one was paying attention. Brad headlined one blog post "Bin Laden Determined to Attack United States" and got four comments. A piece making fun of *Friends* got four hundred.

At a certain point around mid-July, Brad realized there was absolutely no way for him to stop the attacks. The people's indifference to their fate staggered him. *I tried to warn you*, he thought.

He didn't even remember the location of that flight school where the 9/11 attackers had taken their lessons. Sometimes he remembered Florida, other times Arizona, maybe Texas, or possibly Michigan. Besides, even if he could remember, what would he do? Go down there, wait for them to appear, and then punch them out? They'd still get their lessons, and he'd go to jail. He was no action hero. He didn't own a gun. Brad could spend the next two months making hourly panicked calls to the FAA, and those planes would still fly into those towers. Nothing was going to turn him into Jack Ryan or John McClane now.

Certain things about Brad's world were different. He lived in a different city and wore different clothes and had sex with more women and ate at different restaurants on different nights. But history marched on. Everything else was happening in the exact same way in the exact same order. The world seemed indifferent to his slightly altered timeline, swatting it away like a bug. The earth's fate didn't balance on the opinions of a man in his underwear.

The terrible future was going to happen. Brad knew it. But he also knew that the world, while it would become objectively worse for just about everyone for a while, wasn't going to end either. This knowledge just made Brad work harder. He knew his business was going to boom big in the Bush years. There was so much to predict and criticize. If Brad kept pressing, there'd be good gigs.

It wasn't the noblest path, but Brad wasn't the noblest person. He was an ambitious guy who could predict the future. If he couldn't stop 9/11—and he couldn't—then at least he'd have the moral authority to say, "I told you so."

Then he thought about his wife, seriously this time. *Now* he needed her.

Brad had tried really hard to mentally put Juliet away over the years. In his first timeline, she entered the picture in 1997. But on his second try, Brad had won four National Press Club awards by then. He simply wasn't going to wait around. They lived in far-flung neighborhoods, physically and mentally.

But it's not as though Brad had found anyone to replace Juliet either. He didn't even have anyone else he liked to watch TV with.

It was just Brad in his house, in his boxer briefs, typing into the void.

He really started to miss Juliet on their first anniversary, or at least on the day that once had been their first anniversary. On their date they'd gone to an Argentinian steakhouse in Chicago and had their *matrimonio*, a wooden board heaping with grilled meats and vegetables and fried yucca, and then they'd gone to a bad *Star Trek* movie, because that's what Juliet wanted to see, and then they'd gone home and had some more wine and made love, and then Juliet fell asleep while Brad watched *SportsCenter*. Everything they did that night reassured them that they'd married well.

Juliet was such a tender, dear, creative soul, a person of great integrity and wit and depth. Brad had plenty of intelligent and caustic people in his current life, but no one he could trust like Juliet. Even thinking of her maiden name, Loveless, made him sad. Talk about a misnomer! Juliet had been full of love for Brad and the world. And then she'd blithely dismissed him to this terrible fate with her witchly potion. Unless she hadn't. Maybe that had just been some kind of sleep aid. Regardless, he had questions.

Maybe Juliet was still a witch in this timeline too. Brad wanted to find her. He did a search online but found no Juliet Loveless in Chicago. There was one in Alabama, but she turned out to be a hospital dietitian in her early sixties.

But even if Pinterest or Twitter had existed, there was still always the possibility that Juliet had gotten married and changed her last name when he didn't come along, or even opted out of the social media hamster wheel. People did that. It happened. She could even be dead.

Brad called up a reporter colleague in Chicago and asked him to look up Juliet Loveless and J. Loveless in the *White Pages*. There were two listings that fit. Brad kept both the numbers.

On September 11, after the towers came down, Brad talked to his parents and told them he was OK. The phone rang a couple of other times as well. But mostly it was quiet. Washington went into eerie, mournful lockdown when the plane hit the Pentagon, just occasional sirens and the occasional mopey dog walker on the street. Brad was alone. He wanted to be, and it was easy.

Brad knew he needed to start campaigning, however futilely, against the coming Iraq War. The beast needed to be fed. But no one had anything coherent to say or think in the week after 9/11. It was all blather and ideology, a weird mix of elegy and chest thumping. Brad could afford to shut up for a few days until the fog lifted a bit. He let the 9/11 sadness settle onto him like a familiar blanket.

Juliet, he thought.

The first time around they'd comforted each other, maybe a little too much. Their daughter was born nine months later. But there'd been an intimacy to the day, an authentic appreciation of life's tender fragility. LA had only given them *Battlecats*, but at least they had each other. They held each other and cried, terrified of what was coming next. And then they made a baby, an act that always solves life's problems.

Well, this time Brad knew what was next. It wasn't great, admittedly. In fact, it was pretty nightmarish. The next few years would be expensive, violent, corrupt, and really depressing, one of the worst decades in history. But we'd also elect a black president eventually, and people would recognize the right of gay people to marry. The world wasn't going to end quite yet.

Brad wanted to tell Juliet that it was going to be OK, at least for her, as far as he knew.

The first Chicago number, a J. Loveless on Kenmore Avenue, was no longer in service. The second number was for Juliet Loveless on Le Moyne. Brad assumed that was Juliet. How could it be anyone else? She was waiting for him on the North Side.

He dialed. It rang. There was no answer. Brad hung up.

He waited fifteen minutes. By now it was early afternoon, and CNN was nothing but mournful ash filling the screen, anchors weeping openly on air. The national funeral had begun.

Brad called again. Juliet answered on the second ring.

"Hello," she said.

Her voice sounded trembly.

"Hello?" she said again.

"It's going to be OK, Juliet," Brad said.

"What?" Juliet said.

"It's going to be OK."

"Who is this?"

"A friend."

"Seriously, who the hell is this?"

"I . . ." Brad said. "It's going to be OK."

She hung up. Brad called back. The line was busy. He called back. Still busy. Six hours later, he tried again. She answered.

"Hello?" she said.

But Brad didn't have words for Juliet. He reached down with both hands. The phone cord tore out of the wall, splintering wood everywhere.

"Fuck!" Brad shouted.

Juliet wasn't his wife anymore. She never would be in this lifetime. He'd traded her in for a blog. Now he was alone, forever.

Brad walked over to the couch. He sat down and put his head in his hands. For the first time that day, he sobbed.

———

Things got worse before they got better, and then the US invaded Iraq and things got worse again. Either way, business boomed over at Cohenopolis, which is what Brad was calling his website, as the rest of the world gradually got online. Brad took no great pleasure in filing opinionated diatribes on Guantanamo Bay, Abu Ghraib, and the Patriot Act, or lengthy posts describing the creation of the Department of Homeland Security as "the birth of patronage surveillance." But he still posted the opinions at exactly the right point in the media curve. The people were online now, and reading.

What was bad for America was good for the Brad Cohen business. He called the subprime mortgage crisis an "intercontinental boodle quest that made the Teapot Dome look like a Girl Scout Cookies sale" and did so in 2006 when only the true obsessives were paying attention. Meanwhile, his bar mitzvah money continued to marinate in Apple stock, making him a lot of money. He appeared on Bill Maher twice. Jon Stewart asked him, on his third guest appearance, "Why is it that you're always right about everything?" *Time* hired him to write a weekly column.

Brad was on Twitter from Day Ten, on Facebook soon after, and on MSNBC permanently almost immediately after that. *After Dinner with Brad Cohen* premiered to low ratings, until Brad went on a streak in 2006. He started calling Barack Obama "America's first black president," riffing on a phrase that he'd coined in a 1994 *New Century* profile when young Barack was just a community organizer with an eye on the Illinois State Senate. Brad had been cultivating friendships in the Obama camp before that camp had even known it existed.

On election night 2008, Brad sat there on the MSNBC podium alongside Rachel Maddow, Chris Matthews, Big Ed Schultz, and all the other liberal swells, basking in the Dawn of a New America. "Brad," Chris Matthews said, "you got Obama right, you got Hillary right. You got Sarah Palin right. If you'd been alive in 1948, you would have gotten Harry Truman right. I've never seen anyone who's as right as you. So tell us: What's going to happen next?"

"I'm keeping that to myself," Brad said slyly.

Here was the problem, though: Brad didn't know. The statute of limitations was running out on his powers. As of March 2010, his ability to predict the future would expire. Even now he could feel the predictions narrowing away. His mind suffered from a kind of future drought. He knew that Obama would stay in power for at least the next couple of years and that the Republicans would block him at every opportunity, but he had no idea what the outcome of that might be. He couldn't even begin to guess, because he didn't know.

He'd been able to *specifically* predict the 2004 Super Bowl wardrobe malfunction two years ahead of time, but after early 2010, anything that might happen in pop culture was a vast and stupid mystery. Gay marriage rights and legalized marijuana seemed like the right and ethical way to lean, but Brad had no idea where those leanings might lead.

Would Obama get reelected? He didn't know. Where was Osama bin Laden? When would the economy recover? Would the Republicans seize control of both houses of Congress? Would a sinkhole open up and suck the entire state of Kansas into the center of the earth? Would Bono and Bill Gates ascend to heaven together upon a golden chariot drawn by winged horses? Anything was possible. Brad was going to have to learn to fake it like all the other pundits did.

For nearly forty years, Brad been a master of time and had done really well. Now, suddenly he found himself staring into the unknown future. It filled him with dread and fear. His youth was over again, and again he faced the wind down. The universe mocked him with its cruel, infinite unpredictability. He was as screwed as anyone else.

The night before his second fortieth birthday, Brad went for a walk on the National Mall, stoned out of his wits. He tried to think about what would happen tomorrow. Maybe he just needed to wake up, and then clairvoyance would suddenly come to him. But he pretty much knew it wouldn't. He worried that people would soon find out he was a fraud. Somehow he'd have to rally. It wasn't the thought of losing the TV show that bothered him. Honestly, it was kind of a grind, and if he got cut off, he'd almost be grateful. But he didn't want to lose those speaking fees and conference invites. Once the corporate people decided you were smart, the rest of it didn't matter. You could con them for years with techno-babbly motivational talk and hastily sketched "portraits of great men."

Brad meandered home, awash in narcissism. He got to his brownstone. Karen Stafford was waiting for him, wearing a very nice Burberry raincoat and a pair of swank leather boots that came up to her knees. She looked better now than she had in 1992. The Obama years had been good ones in Democratic Washington.

"What are you doing here?" he said.

"It's your birthday," she said.

He and Karen didn't see each other much anymore. They'd tried living together at the end of 2002 and beginning of 2003, five months of wariness and disinterest, and quickly abandoned the project. Now it was the occasional cocktail party or chance meeting at a convention. But once a year she still came by to give Brad his birthday present, which he paid for with a hundred-dollar tip. It was a sick fantasy, and they never told anyone else. Their dynamic only worked if there was a hint of the illicit involved.

"Come on up," he said.

Every year Brad told himself that he was going to stop, that this arrangement was kinky fun in his twenties but that now it was starting to feel desperate. And then every year Karen would pop out of that coat, trimmed as a hedge, and he'd plunge in again. He didn't know what was in it for her exactly. In fact, he'd never bothered to ask, which pretty well summed up the central problem in their relationship.

This year, though, Brad didn't even wait to get up the stairs. He grabbed Karen's shoulder and spun her around. She gasped. Usually she kept him pinned for hours. Brad pressed his mouth against hers. She pushed him away.

"Whoa there, pony," she said. "Aren't you gonna let a girl have a glass of wine first?"

"It's just that . . ." Brad said. "I need . . ."

"Yeah, I know what you need," she said. "Now quit your moaning, take me upstairs, and treat me like a person."

"I can't wait," Brad said.

He relaxed his grip. Karen was the boss. She didn't respond well to aggressive gestures from others. But she'd also misunderstood Brad's urgency. He didn't want to get laid, at least not any more than usual. A feeling welled in his core. He had to express it.

He mounted her the second he had the opportunity, so quickly that neither of them had their tops off. He slid up and down while grunting desperately, a panicked one-way hump.

It only took about a minute. Brad rolled off, peeled away the condom, and panted like a dog. Brad moved up toward her face. He wanted to *cuddle*.

"That was nice," he said.

"Mmm," said Karen.

"I really felt close to you."

Karen propped up on one elbow. "What is wrong with you, Brad?" she said. "You're acting like a wuss."

Brad sighed. "I'm going to be forty," Brad said, "again."

"What do you mean, again?"

"I mean . . ."

Brad couldn't tell her what he meant.

"I don't know who I am after tomorrow."

"You're the talk of Washington," Karen said. "Don't fuck that up now with some ordinary midlife crisis."

"It's not ordinary," he said. "Nothing like this has ever happened to any person."

Karen looked at him disdainfully. Then she looked at her phone.

"I should go," she said. "I'm having breakfast with Elizabeth Warren in about seven hours, and I want to be sharp."

"Fine," Brad said.

Karen was still buttoning her shirt as she walked down the stairs.

A little while later, Brad lay on his Sleep Number mattress, set to seventy-five, while staring at his third-story bedroom skylight, thinking about Juliet. What was she like now? More importantly, had she seen his show?

His daughters, Cori and Claire Cohen, had never been born in this timeline. He hadn't seen them for forty years, and while he was grateful to not have to watch *Wonder Pets!* or *Caillou*, he still missed them. He loved the way Cori would fry ants on the sidewalk with rapt attention for hours, and he even wanted to revisit those god-awful improvised concerts Claire had put on in their living room almost every night. She'd been so full of off-key verve. The girls had given his life substance and meaning at a time when he really didn't have anything else going on.

But he'd completely blown that opportunity. In fact, he hadn't even tried. It made him question if he even wanted to be a dad. Of course he did. But he also, he had to admit, didn't. He liked his freedom now. This was the choice as he saw it: lonely and empty but free, or emotionally fulfilled but trapped.

Brad faced two separate, but also simultaneous, midlives. One of them felt like a movie he'd seen long ago, while the other was more immediate. Either way he had a lot of reckoning ahead.

By most metrics he'd done a better job this time around. He'd played every step smarter, with more confidence. Because of that he was more successful in his career, had a lot more money, owned his house plus a vacation share on Martha's Vineyard, and couldn't walk through an airport, especially not an East Coast airport, without someone stopping and asking him for his autograph. There was little to regret; he was and had been a man of his time.

But the same old dissatisfaction still rose. Only this time he had to face it alone.

What's going to happen to me tomorrow? he wondered.

But Brad wasn't going to find out.

He woke up in the womb.

THE DAILY
DOUBLE

One warm and drizzling May Thursday evening in Brad Cohen's third 2003, he was nursing a porter at a bar on Bedford Avenue in Brooklyn. He'd bought a building in Williamsburg fifteen years earlier, before anyone else was interested, for the price of a Chevy Impala. That was his neighborhood, a good investment.

Interpol and the Strokes were on the juke like in every New York bar in those days. The music stopped. The bartender turned on the TV. A familiar theme played. Everyone in the bar shut up at once.

"Cool," Brad said to the guy next to him. "I love *Jeopardy!*" But he'd mostly forgotten about it in both this life and the last.

"People here are fanatics," the guy said. "They shout out answers, they go nuts. You watch the show?"

"I used to watch it every day," Brad said.

This was the first game of a two-game final for the Tournament of Champions. That meant no "Foods That Start with B" softball categories. Brad found himself growing strangely excited, just like he had in his first go-around in the long-ago days before Alex Trebek shaved his mustache.

The first category that appeared was "The Olympic Games." And the first answer was, "In 1998 she became the youngest person ever to win a gold medal for ladies' figure skating."

"Tara Lipinski," Brad said. One of the contestants on the show guessed Michelle Kwan, another Oksana Baiul. Brad was the only one who was right.

Then it was, "When this US speed skater raced at the 2002 Olympics, his fans sported fake whiskers under their bottom lips."

"Apolo Ohno," Brad said. He'd seen the 2002 Winter Olympics several times. Someone on the game got it right, and so did half the people in the bar.

But Brad also knew that "all roads lead to Rome," that Lennox Lewis won a gold medal boxing for Canada, that the capital of India was New Delhi, that Niels Bohr had been born in Copenhagen, duh, that Bloemfontein was the capital of South Africa, that Jean-Claude Killy was a great French skier, that Hans Blix had been the UN weapons inspector in Iraq in the year 2000, and, for the Daily Double, that Carl Linnaeus of Sweden had coined the term "Homo sapiens" in the eighteenth century.

There had been fifteen questions, and he'd gotten fifteen right.

At the commercial break, the guy next to him said, "You should be on the show."

"Maybe," Brad said.

But of course he should. He was 113 years old. His knowledge went deep and complete. Also, he'd experienced more pop culture than anyone in human history. He was a living VH1 factoid balloon.

Just like in his other iterations, Brad had been born with bad coordination, poor depth perception, and the inability to put together puzzles. That eliminated the possibility of any gig where he worked with his hands. He would never be an architect or mechanic. No matter how hard he practiced or tried, he wasn't going to become a professional baseball player or opera singer. While he liked watching movies about astronauts, he would never *become* one. He simply wouldn't qualify.

But he definitely knew how to read, and this third time through he'd read a lot.

When Brad realized he didn't know anything about British kings, he read about British kings. If it occurred to him that he didn't understand the terms "mitosis" and "meiosis," he'd go to the library and read about cell division until he figured it out. He read all of Trollope and all of Proust, and then he learned some French so that he could read Proust again in the original. He also became proficient in Spanish, Hebrew, Latin, Russian, Arabic, Farsi, Portuguese, Mandarin, and Hindi, with little dustings of Dutch and Gaelic. And that was all before he turned twenty-one (the third time).

Brad spent these '90s auditing classes at Columbia University and NYU, learning everything he could about Hinduism, Buddhism, objectivism, the history of the Ottoman Empire, sixteenth-century poetry, jazz history, African geography, Italian idioms, Canadian politics, the Bloomsbury Group, the Gadsden Purchase, German cinema, and, given that this was the go-go age of political correctness, more than his fair share of postcolonial feminist literary theory.

He went deep into theoretical physics and organic chemistry and invertebrate anatomy. He learned BASIC and FORTRAN and Hypertext and Pascal. When Java debuted at Sun Microsystems in 1995, Brad was on top of it right away. From Newton's laws of motion to the history of Protestantism, from the works of W. E. B. Du Bois to Hammurabi's laws, he was a student of everything.

And now he knew all the answers on *Jeopardy!*

After the commercial, Brad answered that David Mamet wrote *Speed-the-Plow*, that Pete Seeger wrote "Turn! Turn! Turn!" and that the answer to "This adjective referring to the works of G. B. S. is derived from the Latinized form of his surname" is "Shavian." He also correctly identified the French term *roman à clef*. The final answer of the round was "Mount Gay Rum has been made in this West Indies island nation off northeastern South America for three hundred years."

"What is Barbados?" Brad said correctly.

There had been thirty questions. Brad had known the answer to all thirty of them. He knew all thirty in the second round too.

For *Final Jeopardy!*, the bar passed around slips of paper for everyone to write their answers. Anyone who answered correctly got a free well shot. The category was "Governors," and the question went, "In 1967 she became the first woman governor of a state east of the Mississippi River."

"Jesus *Christ*," said the bartender.

There were about twenty people playing at the bar. Half of them immediately crumpled up their papers and threw them to the ground. Others just stared at the paper blankly or scratched their chins as the traditional *Final Jeopardy!* music played its little singsong, music-box, thirty-seconds-of-doom theme: *Dah dah dah dah dah dah DAH—dah dah dah dah dum de dum di dum dum.*

This was trivia. It was *trivial*. Brad tapped his foot under the bar.

He wrote down "Bella Abzug" but immediately crossed it out because he knew she'd never been a governor. So he wrote down something else.

Time expired. One of the contestants wrote down "Who is Ferraro?" That was wrong. Another wrote "Who is Brown?," hoping that picking a common last name would allow him to stumble into the answer. The third wrote down "Who is Bella Abzug?" Also wrong. This was, in *Jeopardy!* parlance, a Triple Stumper.

The correct answer was Lurleen B. Wallace of Alabama. The entire bar groaned.

No one even bothered to show their napkins. Except Brad. He flipped his over. It said "Lurleen B. Wallace." He'd known the answer. He'd known *every* answer.

"Hell, man," said the bartender, "have a premium drink. Not just a shot."

"How about Mount Gay Rum?" Brad said.

"You got it."

Brad quaffed that Potent Potable and seven more. He staggered home to his Williamsburg loft, which, when he'd bought it in 1991, had boasted a view of a garbage scow and the Twin Towers. Now the scow had been removed, the docks were being renovated, and the towers were a hole in the ground. He'd watched them come down on September 11, once again powerless to affect history.

But suddenly life number three had a purpose. Brad had found a sport. He wasn't just going to go on *Jeopardy!* He was going to go on *Jeopardy!* and win. But he wasn't just going to win. He was going to win a lot.

There would be no more drinking, no more pot smoking, no more anything but careful study and hard preparation. Brad already knew more about everything than anyone else in the world, but he needed to know even more.

"Juliet," he said. "You'll be proud of me."

He said that to the air, because Juliet wasn't there. She hadn't been there in almost eighty years. Brad spoke to no one, because he had no one.

He was extremely lonely and extremely rich. These were the perfect conditions under which to enter the *Jeopardy!* dojo. He had no earthly distractions.

Brad was going to be the greatest game-show contestant of all time.

———

Six months later Brad walked into a basement room at the Westin in Midtown Manhattan for his *Jeopardy!* audition. He arrived more than a half hour before his call time, yet there were nearly two hundred people milling about a chandeliered, windowless ante-chamber, many of them sitting nervously in metal-backed hotel chairs, talking in low tones to their spouses or their mothers or their trusted friends. They'd come from as far as Florida and Ohio. Most of them would be rejected by the show on the spot. But Brad pitied them less than those who did make it onto the show. They would be crushed by his juggernaut. His reign would last a thousand episodes.

"Where you in from?" Brad heard someone say behind him.

He turned. "Huh?" Brad said.

He saw a big-shouldered man, late thirties, wearing the epaulets and tight polyester uniform of the United States Air Force.

"Did you have to travel far?"

"Oh, no," Brad said. "I live over in Brooklyn."

"Brooklyn, huh? I hear it's getting pretty popular."

You have no idea who you're up against, Brad thought.

"Yep," Brad said. "Pretty popular."

"Well, I'm up from Fort Bragg, North Carolina. Got a three-day leave, and I thought I'd see the city."

What a hillbilly, Brad thought.

"Yeah, I haven't been here since I got my master's in international economics from Columbia," he said.

Well played.

This was *Jeopardy!* You didn't even try unless you were smart.

Brad extended his hand. "Good luck today," he said.

"You too," said Air Force, gripping Brad firmly. Too firmly. It hurt. The game had already begun.

Doors opened. Out stepped a woman in her late forties wearing a flowing caftan and a pair of slippers, not exactly what Brad had expected.

"Good morning!" exclaimed the woman.

"G'mrning," the crowd mumbled sheepishly like a bunch of shy and angry middle schoolers.

The woman looked disappointed.

"*Good morning!*" she said, raising her eyebrows wide and lifting her palms to indicate that this crowd needed to bring up the energy.

"*Good morning!*" everyone said, this time *too* enthusiastically.

The woman waved her bescarved arms like a shopping-mall Stevie Nicks.

"Who here is ready to play *Jeopardy!*?" she exclaimed.

The crowd had caught on. They whistled, hooted, and applauded. Brad joined them. This *was* exciting after all.

"Good!" she said. "My name is Barbara Stevens. I'm one of the *Jeopardy!* contestant coordinators. Hopefully, you'll all be seeing a lot more of me. Well . . ."

She held out her arms wide.

"Maybe not *more* of me. But at least more often."

This got a lot of laughter. She grinned broadly, theatrically, Auntie Mame welcoming befuddled dinner guests. Then, just as dramatically, she made a sad face.

"Unfortunately, most of you won't," she said.

That quieted the nervous titters.

"That's just the way things work in *Jeopardy!*-land," she said. "If I had my choice, you would all be champions. But we have to winnow the field somehow. So this is how it's going to work. I'm going to take you into *that* room . . ." She pointed behind her, from whence she'd emerged. "My friends and I are going to give you ten

Jeopardy! answers. And you're going to have to give us the questions very fast. The whole thing is going to take about a minute for each of you. When it's over, we'll tabulate the scores and post them up on this wall. Only thirty-five of you will be returning after lunch."

"How many do we have to get correct?" asked a mousy-looking girl wearing a University of Iowa sweatshirt.

"Honey," she said maternally, "if I were you, I'd try to get *all* of them right."

She looked out at the crowd. "The same goes for all of you!" she said. "This is the big leagues, but I think you all are ready. Most of all remember: it's a *game.* Have *fun.*"

Brad looked around. A few people were beaming openly. They *were* having fun. That was good. They could keep having fun. Right until the moment he garroted them onstage with his insanely comprehensive brain knowledge, the collected wisdom of twelve decades.

He pulled a slip of paper out of his pocket. On it was a maxim from Sun Tzu that he'd been using to motivate himself. It read: "Engage people with what they expect; it is what they are able to discern and confirms their projections. It settles them into predictable patterns of response, occupying their minds while you wait for the extraordinary moment—that which they cannot anticipate."

Brad was ready for war.

———

They took the contestants in alphabetical order. The first, a lawyer from Philly named Abrams, went in; ninety seconds later she emerged looking like digested sausage.

"I totally froze," she said. "I could only answer maybe three of those questions. They asked them so fast. It was confusing."

She walked toward the bar, muttering to herself. Brad breathed deeply. They called on him less than a quarter hour later.

He went into the room and stood at a podium. Fifteen feet in front of him, Barbara Stevens sat at a conference table. On her left sat a man, probably fifteen years younger, and 100 percent more Filipino, and on her right sat an African American woman, midthirties, nerdy looking, like just about everyone in *Jeopardy!*-land.

"Brad Cohen," Barbara said, "of Brooklyn, New York. We're going to give you ten answers. You have to get as many of the questions right as you possibly can. Your maximum allowed time is ninety seconds . . . *total*. Do you think you can do it?"

"I know I can," Brad said.

Barbara laughed in a tone equal parts total empathy and pure disdain.

"Confidence," she said. "That's what I like to hear. Let's begin."

Barbara and her two assistants read off questions rapid-fire, almost slurring the words. It was a script they'd seen a hundred times before. *Jeopardy!* had given him no hints. He just had to know everything. Fortunately, he did.

"Who is Keats?"

"What is Sri Lanka?"

"What is Destiny's Child?"

"What is Lexus?"

"Who is Winnie the Pooh?"

"What were the 1890s?"

"Who is Charlemagne?"

"Who were Ali and Foreman?"

"What is the liver?"

"What is *Doctor Zhivago*?"

One of Barbara's assistants slapped on a stopwatch.

"Sixty-one seconds," he said.

Barbara's face scrunched into approval. "That's pretty fast," she said. "But did you get them all right?"

"I got them all right," Brad said.

"How do you know?"

Because I'm old enough to be your great-grandfather, Brad thought, but instead he said, "I know."

For the rest of the morning, Brad sat in the atrium, watching people come out of the room looking shattered. A few seemed confident. Finally, after Donald Ziriax emerged saying "I fucked that" and walking straight into the lobby and onto Fifth Avenue, it was over. They waited another fifteen minutes, and then one of Barbara's assistants posted the callback list on the door to the conference room. There was a bum rush. Some people whooped. Others turned away silently, heads down. A mother patted her son's back and said, "You'll get it next year." Brad's name was on the list, right at the top.

Barbara emerged flowingly, like Gloria Swanson coming down the staircase in *Sunset Boulevard*. She grinned.

"OK!" she said. "Are you excited?"

"Yes!" said the remaining thirty-five people.

Barbara sighed. "I said, *are you excited*?"

Yes! Wahoo! Whoop. Applause.

"That's better," she said. "I'm excited too. Why?"

She made a little inch sign with her thumb and index finger. "Because I'm this much closer to going up to my hotel room and soaking my feet. But beyond that, I'm excited because we've narrowed it down. Here's the good news: you all did the best on our pop quiz. And now you're officially in the *Jeopardy!* contestant pool."

Dreams did come true in America. They were coming true right now.

"But just because you're in the pool doesn't mean that you're going to get to swim," Barbara said. "You've got to show us exactly what you can do."

After an hour-and-a-half lunch break, the doors opened. First, they took a hundred-question test. Brad knew the answers. Then it was time to face the theme music. They would play simulated games with simulated buzzers, the equivalent of taking live batting practice against an actual pitcher.

They got called up in threes. Brad felt himself instinctively clicking on his pen. The longer the day went, the more nervous he felt. His confidence cracked slightly. Suddenly, he *wanted* this. Minutes passed slowly.

"Brad Cohen," he heard someone call.

"Huh?" he said, looking up.

"It's your turn," Barbara said. She gave him a little smirk.

He hustled up to the podium. Next to him were the air force guy he'd talked to before and a college admissions counselor from Bethlehem, Pennsylvania.

Barbara said, "Brad, tell us about yourself."

Well, Brad thought, *I've been born three times, but every time I'm about to turn forty, I get reborn as a fully sentient baby. That makes me nearly 114 years old on a human scale. I was the editor of the* New Century *magazine and a pundit on MSNBC and also a failed screenwriter. And if this scenario doesn't work out, I'll probably get born again and have to spend another two years sucking on my mother's tit.*

But that's not what he said, because he didn't want them to call security on him. Instead, he said, "I'm an independent scholar from right here in New York City."

"What does that mean, independent scholar?" asked Richard the contestant coordinator.

"I audit classes at universities."

"What kinds of classes?"

"Whatever I'm interested in. Right now I'm missing a graduate seminar on the history of industrial-era Britain."

"Sorry to make you miss the class."

"That's OK," Brad said. "It's pretty boring."

"But how do you make your living, Brad?" Barbara asked.

"I invested my bar mitzvah money in the stock market, and it's gone pretty well from there," Brad said.

The crowd laughed.

Brad said, "I'm serious. I've never had a job."

In this lifetime, he thought grimly.

"First time I've ever heard that," Barbara said. "Are you married?"

No, Brad thought. *Yes. Maybe.*

"I used to be," he said.

"I'll ask no more questions," said Barbara.

"I appreciate it."

It was time for Brad's sample game.

"Brad, you get to pick first," Barbara said.

"OK," he said. "I'll take Literary Birthplaces for two hundred."

Barbara said, "I'll name the fictional character. You have to name where they were born."

The first clue was "Tiny Tim."

Brad pounded the buzzer. He didn't get in. The air force guy did and answered "London" correctly. Air Force bopped over to Potent Potables for two hundred and nailed down "gin." A half-dozen questions passed. Brad wasn't having any luck. He smacked the buzzer hard like a car horn and caressed it softly like a kitten. Nothing could get it to respond.

"Brad, you're coming in too early," Barbara said.

"OK," Brad said.

"Sports Stadiums for six," the college admissions counselor said.

The answer was simply Tropicana Field.

Brad hit the buzzer. He saw a light.

"Brad?" Barbara said.

"What is Tampa?" Brad said, and then he was off. He knew that Uncle Tom from *Uncle Tom's Cabin* had been born in Kentucky, and that George VI was Queen Elizabeth II's father.

Then he hit Potent Potables: "What is a Tom Collins?"

"What is mescal?"

"What is rum?"

The buzzer hummed in his hand. He fingered it like a . . . *like a clitoris*, he thought. *No, wait, that's sexist. But it's also true.*

It *was* a trivia clitoris. And he was its master. Brad Cohen, the king of the trivia clit.

Six weeks later, his phone rang.

"Brad," said the voice on the other end. "It's Barbara from *Jeopardy!*"

"I've been waiting for you to call," he said.

"I bet you have," she said. "You cocky bastard."

"Well?" Brad said.

"Well, how'd you like to be on the show?"

"I'd like that a lot."

"Your episode is taping in five weeks. Can you make it out to LA for that?"

"Of course."

"You'll have to pay for your own plane ticket. We have a hotel discount near the studio for the contestants."

"Not a problem."

"I figured it wouldn't be for an independently wealthy bar mitzvah money investor."

"It wouldn't be, and it isn't."

"You're a strange guy, Brad Cohen."

"Don't I know it?" Brad said.

"Alex won't know what to make of you."

"He'll have to make a lot of me when I keep winning."

"Most people lose," she said. "That's the way it goes. We tape five episodes a day."

"I won't lose."

"I admire your confidence. You got every single one of the answers right on the practice test. That doesn't happen very often. But it all evens out on taping day."

"We'll see."

"That we will. We'll be mailing you an orientation packet today. And then we'll see you on the twenty-first."

"And the twenty-second," Brad said. "And the twenty-third."

"We only tape two days a week," she said.

"OK," Brad said. "The twenty-eighth then."

And all summer long.

Five weeks later Brad Cohen lay in bed in his fifth-floor room at the DoubleTree in Culver City, California. To reduce noise, he'd asked for a room on one of the top floors, away from the 405, which the hotel faced on one side. His bedside clock said 4:15 a.m. Even though he'd been out like Snow White at 8:30 p.m., he still hadn't gotten eight hours.

There was a plastic bottle of water on the bedside table, warm to the touch. Brad sat up and gulped the entire bottle. Then he stood, stretched, went to the window, and opened the drapes. A garbage truck moved down Sepulveda. Parking-lot lights illuminated the Dinah's Fried Chicken sign. A slender crack of gray began to spread across the horizon. This was it. The day he was going to tape *Jeopardy!*

Brad dropped to the ground and did twenty quick push-ups, and then another ten not as quickly. His breathing was more labored than he would have liked. So he sat still, like they'd taught him to at the Brooklyn Zen Academy, where he'd taken meditation classes in preparation.

In his mind he sat at the center of a cone of brilliant white light. Everything around him was one—all the noise, all his thoughts, the stained carpet beneath the pillow he was sitting on—a unified field of awareness.

He put on some sweatpants and went downstairs. There was a Starbucks in the lobby just opening for the day at 5:15 a.m. Brad ordered the first pour. He sat in a lounge chair and sipped it, feeling strangely nervous. In his last incarnation he'd appeared on TV hundreds of times, usually live. But this was different. This was the Super Bowl.

Upstairs, he took a shower, shaved, and packed a duffel. They'd asked him to bring a change of outfits in case he appeared on more than one episode. He'd packed ten outfits, including three different sports coats, in two different suitcases. Of *course* he'd appear on more than one episode. He picked one, camel's hair, or at least *fake* camel's hair, a light blue shirt, and a black tie, no pattern, like they'd asked.

By that time it was 7:15 a.m. Room service knocked. They'd brought him a glass of orange juice, a bowl of fruit, and a spinach, mushroom, and cheese omelet. He was disappointed to see that they'd left off his side of avocado. That really would have helped.

It was good for the mind.

———

Two hours later the contestant shuttle bus pulled up inside a covered parking area on the Sony lot. The passengers got out, Brad included, like clowns exiting the world's most intellectual circus car. All of them had suitcases or duffels or garment bags full of dress clothes. They stood in a glass enclosure waiting to be sacrificed in the Brainiac Thunderdome.

Ten minutes passed. Fifteen. The small talk had been exhausted. They just wanted to play, to get their hands on the buzzers, to see the board, to stare into the face of Trebek.

Finally, a man appeared, midforties, big smile, dressed not too fancy.

"I'm Jeremy Wolf," he said, "the lead contestant coordinator. I've had this job for fifteen years, so I can tell you the answer to all your questions: no, yes, no, and Alex is not going to grow his mustache back."

That got a nice laugh.

"So are you all ready to play *Jeopardy!*?"

"*Yes!*" the contestants, including Brad, all responded.

They knew the drill by now.

"Good," he said. "Come with me."

They walked maybe twenty feet. There it stood, Sony Pictures Studios Stage 10. A six-thousand-foot-tall talismanic photo of Alex Trebek watched over the lot like a benevolent Canadian god.

They passed through a metal detector and put their bags through an X-ray machine. As they went through a side door, Brad craned his neck to get a glimpse of the set, and so did everyone else, but Jeremy Wolf kept them together, like the sheep his namesake liked to eat. Brad got a faint glimpse of a glass case containing many Emmys and photos and memorabilia.

They were in a green room. It wasn't technically green, more a lightish blue, but it was a "greenroom," a waiting area for the Johnny Gilbert–narrated apocalypse. There were buckets of soda cans and plastic iced tea and carafes of coffee, a huge plastic catered dish of fruit, and another full of cardboard-looking Danishes, bombs of jelly and frosting that were bad for the brain. There were fifteen contestants and four contestant coordinators. They sat at a long conference table, while a few more sat on couches. All of them had clipboards.

Brad had signed his name fewer times when he was applying for a housing loan. There were tax forms and nondisclosure agreements and forms to agree that he understood the rules. He also had to fill out some chatty information forms, including the dreaded "personal anecdotes."

Brad had to choose three interesting things to say about himself. The most interesting thing—the fact that he was, apparently, caught forever in an *infinite time loop*—would be rejected out of hand and would probably get him thrown off the show. Most of his other good anecdotes, like when he'd insulted Newt Gingrich in an elevator or traveled to Berlin two days before the wall fell, sounded equally unbelievable and were all related to the first part. He couldn't talk to Alex about how he'd met his wife, because he'd met her more than eighty years ago, and even though she was probably alive now, she wasn't going to know who he was. And he couldn't talk about his daughters, the oldest of whom, Claire, would only have been two years old in his normal timeline but didn't exist in this one. That was a decidedly untrivial fact.

So he played it safe, saying that his first word was "Elvis," that he'd invested his bar mitzvah money in Apple stock, and he also added that he'd met Mike Ditka when he was a kid. The third wasn't actually true from any lifetime, but it also wasn't checkable.

One of the contestant coordinators came by and looked at Brad's sheet, nodding in approval. "Alex will like all of those," he said.

The morning's carbohydrate and coffee highs had worn off. Everyone in the room was chattering and shaking nervously. *Are you ready to play the Hunger Games?* Brad thought but didn't say, because *The Hunger Games* was still more than three years away from publication, and Suzanne Collins was still working as a writer for *Clifford's Puppy Days*. Now *there* was someone who turned a children's TV career into success. Brad wondered if he could have parlayed *Battlecats* better. If only he'd had better management, better luck, and more talent.

Eighty years on, and he was still bitter about failing in Hollywood.

This is what Brad remembered, and hated, about the entertainment business: the endless waiting in chairs. You waited and waited. Then someone finally appeared, flashed a smile, offered you a bottle of water, and crushed your dreams.

Not this time, though.

Screw you, Hollywood, Brad thought. *Today I get my revenge.*

He would reclaim his dignity.

On a game show.

The door flung open. Barbara Stevens flowed in on a cloud.

"Good morning, my little flowers!" she exclaimed.

"Good morning!" her little flowers exclaimed back nervously.

"Now I know you're all excited to get out there and to see the set," Barbara said. "But there are some rules we've got to explain."

They didn't turn out to be rules so much. Everyone knew the rules. They were more like maxims for *Jeopardy!* success. The first, Barbara said, was "Play your game." In other words, stick with whatever strategy you had when you arrived.

"Rule number two," Barbara said, was "don't get flustered!"

That was a laugh. The entire experience down to the arctic blast of the air-conditioning seemed to exist *precisely* to fluster.

"Rule number three," Barbara said, "get your timing down!"

"Timing." Here was the key to it all, the only thing that mattered. You weren't allowed to buzz in until Alex Trebek was done reading the question. Even then there was a microcosmic delay before a set of lights (invisible to the home viewer) on either side of the question board blinked on. If you clicked the buzzer before then, you got locked out for a quarter of a second. If you clicked too much after that, a competitor would beat you to the answer.

"It's a high-wire coordination act," Barbara said. "I won't lie to you. One time we had a guy who hired two occupational therapists. He trained with them for weeks. His thumb muscles were *huge*. They looked like chicken drumsticks. Remember that movie *Even Cowgirls Get the Blues*, with Uma Thurman?"

"Based on a Tom Robbins novel," said a guy at the table.

Barbara touched her index finger to her nose.

"Very *good*, Colin," she said, "but save it for the game. In any case, this guy came in, and he was *ready* for the buzzer. He was going to destroy it. Anyone want to guess what happened to him?"

"He won?" a young woman said sheepishly.

"He *should* have won," Barbara said. "His buzzer strategy was great. But he missed *Final Jeopardy!*, so he lost. This is a cruel game. Isn't that right, Brad?"

She remembers me, Brad thought. Why single him out? It didn't matter. This was all part of the game.

"I don't know," Brad said. "I haven't played it yet."

"That's the right answer!" Barbara said. "And also the wrong one. *Jeopardy!* is definitely a hard game. But it's also fun! Remember this above everything else: you made it! You're here! It's going to happen! So have fun."

Around the table, everyone looked pale and terrified. Brad felt his confidence wane just a little. It felt less like a game show and more like the antechamber to a mass execution, with pictures of Alex Trebek on the walls. One of the contestants, a "project systems administrator" from suburban Chicago, stood up and ran to a bathroom.

A door slammed. The man wretched, audible even over the loud bathroom fan. Everyone sat uncomfortably, waiting for it to end. The man emerged, looking sheepish. The right collar of his button-down shirt was a little wet.

"Sorry," he said. "Too much coffee."

"Nothing to apologize for, Gary," Barbara said. "It happens all the time."

A few more seconds passed. Brad drilled his fingers on the table. Over on the couches, contestant coordinators shuffled through papers.

"OK then," Barbara said. "Who wants to see the set?"

———

They beheld Oz in all its splendor. The set glistened, all purples and blues and oranges and reds. Whoever designed the color scheme must have really liked '70s and '80s Hot Wheels.

Three podiums sat in a line, the word "Jeopardy!" behind them. The board went floor to ceiling, enormous, no dollar spared there. There were cameras all around, big ones, just to remind everyone: you're going to be on TV.

The contestants stepped onto the gleaming molded-plastic stage, as wary as cows being let out of the barn after a long winter. Barbara had disappeared for some sort of meeting, or maybe to smoke a cigarette out on the lot. Jeremy Wolf, the guy who'd met them out in the parking garage, herded them. They'd been there almost three hours. The morning's excitement had been replaced by numbness. Brad's brain felt slow, but his heart was cranking.

Deep breath, Cohen, he thought to himself. *Don't be stupid. Your moment has arrived. You are a golden god of knowledge.*

Jeremy Wolf wrangled them all behind the podia.

"This is where you're all going to stand," he said. "Hopefully, some of you will stand here for a while."

I will stand as champion forever, Brad said to himself.

And then, just like that, it was time to play.

Contestants were chosen by random draw. Brad didn't get picked for the first game. Instead, he had to watch the returning champion, a DC lawyer, mince apart a "systems account supervisor from Chillicothe, Ohio," and a graduate student of history from Falls Church, Virginia. Then that game was over, and the lawyer was $23,900 wealthier. The contestant coordinators didn't call Brad's name, again, for game two.

Brad sat in his chair, nervously pressing his thumb against his thigh. How was he going to master the buzzer? How was he going to remember everything he knew, from all his lifetimes? The lights were hot, even in the seats. He was sweating.

Game two went fast. The lawyer dominated again, but not as much, and he didn't have an insurmountable lead going into the final. The question was, "In 1913, this alloy was invented by Harry Brearley of Sheffield, England, a city known for its cutlery since before 1400." Brad knew the answer immediately. The third-place contestant drew a total blank, bet all of his $5,500, and shanked his way ignominiously out of *Jeopardy!* history. The second-place contestant, a systems administrator from Fort Worth, Texas, got the question right. She answered, "What is stainless steel?" but incomprehensibly only bet $100 of her $10,500.

Still, it proved smart, or lucky, because the champion wrote down, "What is tin?" He missed the question and lost a lot of money on a big bet. His run was done.

"But we'll see you in the Tournament of Champions," Alex said to the lawyer.

Pick me now, Brad thought. *Oh, please. I'm so very ready.*

Everything was lined up. Brad would face a weak champion. He was going to knock it out.

"Brad?" he heard faintly.

And then again, *"Brad!"*

"What?"

"It's your turn," Barbara said.

"Oh!" Brad said.

"Well, hustle, soldier," she said. "We're on a schedule. They're waiting for you in makeup."

Brad bolted out of his seat and ran back to the greenroom. He really had to pee.

———

A few minutes later, Brad was on set. A makeup lady patted him with a puff. There were three cameras facing him dead-on, with an entire football field between him and the lenses.

"When we introduce you," Jeremy Wolf said, "look at the middle one. And just relax into it. This is a game. Enjoy yourself. It'll be over soon."

The cameras were rolling. Johnny Gilbert introduced the young woman to his left, a stenographer from Park City, Utah. Then he said, "An independent scholar and investor from Brooklyn, New York. Brad Cohen!"

Brad smiled wanly. He had a headache. Johnny introduced the champion, who was still administering systems in Texas. Alex Trebek appeared, looking smooth as ever.

"Thank you, Johnny," he said, "and hello, everybody. Our returning champion, Sarah, made a savvy bet on *Final Jeopardy!* yesterday. And she got the question right to boot. That's why she's here today. And she's going to try to do it again. Brad and Kori might have something to say about that. Let's go to the board and see what happens."

The categories revealed themselves: Literary Collaborators, Poker Face, Pour Me a Stiff One, "Court" Briefs, Talk Like a Brit, and 'Allo, Governor!

"Sarah, make your selection."

"I'll take Literary Collaborators for two hundred dollars, Alex," said the returning champ.

Alex read suavely, "These brothers first published their fairy tales in 1812 as *Kinder- und Hausmärchen*."

Brad hit the buzzer. He saw, from his side of the podium, the light come on.

"Brad?" said Trebek.

"Who are the Brothers Grimm?" Brad said, and he was off and running, ready to play his game. He was going to find the Daily Double early, rack up the points, and leave his opponents gasping.

"Literary Collaborators for eight hundred dollars," he said.

"OK," Alex said, and then read, "Sidney Howard helped this author dramatize *Dodsworth*."

Again, Brad blew in fast. He saw the lights.

"Brad," Trebek said again.

"Who is Dickens?" Brad said.

"Oh no," Trebek said, his voice dropping. Brad saw his number slip to minus six hundred. He was in the red. The dreaded red.

Sinclair Lewis! Brad thought to himself. He'd known the right answer. But he had choked legitimately. He needed to slow down.

Brad picked again.

"Literary Collaborators for one thousand dollars," he said.

"George S. Kaufman died in June 1961," Trebek read. "This man, his frequent collaborator, in December that year."

Brad hit the buzzer. The lights went off.

"Brad?" Alex said.

Brad knew the answer. He *knew* it. But there were lights. Alex Trebek stared at him from behind the podium. Brad couldn't remember. What was the name? The *name*!

"Who is Groucho Marx?" he said timidly, credulously, knowing that he was wrong.

"Incorrect," Alex said.

Neither of the opponents buzzed in. The answer was "Moss Hart."

"After three clues," Alex said, "Brad has negative sixteen hundred. The other players each have zero. Maybe someone will answer something correctly before the game is over."

Burn!

"Brad," Trebek said. "Pick again."

Brad's initial strategy had failed. He was going to have to play slowly and build his money back up.

"Poker Face for two hundred dollars," he said.

At the commercial break, after fifteen questions, Brad was still at negative six hundred. He'd correctly answered that Stoli is a brand of vodka and had correctly identified the face of Catherine Zeta-Jones. No one was impressed by his intellectual juggernaut. Brad sat in third place, his dreams heading down the bowl in a very slow flush.

At the break, Trebek came over. Everyone got a picture with the great man. Trebek put his arm around Brad as the camera snapped.

"Not as easy as you thought, eh?" he said.

"I'll figure it out," Brad said.

"We'll see."

Curse you, Trebek!

Then came the theme music, and it was time for the awkward "contestant interaction" portion of the show.

Brad Cohen has been born three times and is apparently cursed to live the first 40 years of his life over and over again until he figures out how to escape the cycle. He's now 114 years old. Brad, what is that like?

Well, it's not easy, Alex . . .

"Brad Cohen, an independent scholar from Brooklyn," Alex said. "What does that mean exactly?"

"Well, I audit classes at various universities to try and learn as much as I can," Brad said.

"That should help you on *Jeopardy!*" said Trebek, "ostensibly."

Double burn!

While Brad hemmed, Trebek asked him, "So how can you afford to do this? Don't you have to work?"

"Well, that's personal, Alex," Brad said, "but if you have to know, I invested my bar mitzvah money wisely twenty years ago, so I can devote my life to learning—and to becoming a *Jeopardy!* champion."

"We'll see," Trebek said again.

He made everything ominous.

Brad had $800 at the end of the first round. His opponents were doing fine. One had $3,500, and the other was at $5,200.

Brad took a deep breath.

No, I am not going to lose, he thought. *Not today. Not ever.*

Brad got first pick in *Double Jeopardy!* He went straight for the $2,000 clue in "Science Briefs." The clue was, "When the stork won't come: IVF." He knew the right question was "What is in vitro fertilization?" But he couldn't get the buzzer to work, and the champ got in ahead of him.

Dammit.

Dammit!

Before Brad knew it, he was down almost ten grand and there were only twenty clues left. Brad got "Who is Captain Nemo?" for $400 and "What is Captain Blood?" for $2,000, and then he went for "Shakespearean Words" at $2,000.

The Daily Double alarm sounded. This was it! Brad's moment.

"Brad," Trebek said, "you have three thousand two hundred dollars. You can't take the lead. But you can move closer. What's your wager going to be?"

Brad wound up, and then he said: "Let's make it a true Daily Double, Alex."

The audience actually *gasped*. Brad was putting on a show. He would give them their free ticket's worth.

"OK," Alex said. "For three thousand two hundred dollars, here goes: 'The word "fashionable" came into vogue with Achilles's speech to Ulysses in this play.'"

Brad had read Shakespeare. He'd read all the Shakespeare. He knew everything about it. And he definitely knew this answer. Achilles and Ulysses only appeared in one play.

"What is *Troilus and Cressida*?" he said.

"You are correct," said Alex Trebek.

That was a champion's answer. Brad was still in third, but it was a competitive third. Unfortunately, he was *still* in third place when the game ended. He had $9,200. The returning champ had $11,400. And the other contestant was at $10,200.

"It's a close game," Trebek said, "and it's all going to come down to our contestants' knowledge of this category."

He turned to his right. On a screen next to him, a word appeared in white block letters on a royal-blue background: "Cartoons."

Brad wrote down $9,200 as his bet. He was letting it ride.

Five minutes passed. Trebek did a couple of retakes. The theme music played, the red lights went on, and Trebek said, "Close game today. All three contestants are in a good position. But it all comes down to their knowledge of this category, cartoons. Here's the clue."

It appeared. Trebek read, "This Canadian action cartoon from the '80s had an unsuccessful twenty-five-episode reboot in 2002."

Could it be? Really?

"What is *Battlecats*?" Brad wrote.

The music ended. Alex approached the contestants.

"Was it an easy question? Or a hard one? Let's see," he said. "Brad wrote . . ."

And the monitor revealed, "'What is *Battlecats*?'" Alex said, "And he is absolutely right. From my home country, the reboot was a bust and featured some disastrously bad writing."

True enough, Brad thought.

"And let's see what he wagered: everything he had, bringing him up to eighteen thousand four hundred dollars."

The contestant in the middle guessed, "What is He-Man?"

"I'm sorry," Alex Trebek said. "He-Man wasn't Canadian."

Truer words were never spoken.

"It all comes down to our champion," said Trebek. "What did she write down as her response?"

Brad held his breath.

"What is GI Joe?"

He let his breath out.

"I'm sorry, that is also incorrect," Trebek said. "And what was her wager? Everything she had. And that means that with eighteen thousand four hundred dollars, Brad Cohen of Brooklyn, New York, is the new *Jeopardy!* champion!"

There was applause. The camera closed in tightly on Brad's face. He smiled. He also felt sick. He was going to win a hundred games in a row.

Brad walked off the stage, swaying his hips from side to side. His balls would have made a beautiful noise if they'd been made of brass.

"Congratulations, champ," one of the camera guys said to him, shaking his hand.

On the way back to the dressing room, people praised him:

"Way to go, champ."

"Good work, champ."

And, simply, "*Battlecats*. Nice."

Jeremy Wolf came up to him and said, "Man, I thought you were going down in flames."

The universe had sent Brad a message, and that message was: you are a *Jeopardy!* champion.

Barbara Stevens entered. "Brad!" she said.

"I *told* you I was going to win," he said.

"You were right," she said.

"And I'm going to win again," he said.

Brad waited for something else. Nothing else came. Barbara was not impressed. Yet.

"First you have to go eat lunch," she said.

———

Brad won his second game against a couple of easily intimidated cupcakes, bringing in more than thirty-one grand.

But in his third game, the lawyer from Smyrna, Georgia, who stood to his left, had him by the scruff from the opening signal. His reactions were slow, and his recall dull. Brad felt cooked, and he played that way. He shanked questions about the Macy's Thanksgiving Day parade, the Chrysler Building, George Sand, and Franz Schubert. Strangely, he ran a category about birds, including a big-money Daily Double, which left him with $7,500, in third place. He still had a chance to win. The *Final Jeopardy!* category was "New York City."

Brad bet it all.

The question went, "Opened in 1937, it got its name in response to the George Washington Bridge, north of it."

Brad knew the answer right away.

"What is the Lincoln Tunnel?" he wrote.

And he was right. He had fifteen grand.

But the other two contestants got it right as well. Brad finished in third place.

Alex Trebek shook his hand after the show was over.

"Better luck next time," he said.

"I'm caught in an infinite time loop!" Brad blurted. "It's forcing me to live the first forty years of my life over and over again!"

It felt good to tell someone at last.

Alex Trebek patted him on the shoulder. "I know the feeling," he said. "I have to tape five more of these fuckers tomorrow."

Brad stepped off the stage. They handed him a couple of yellow slips of paper, indicating how much money he'd won.

"You'll get your check about four months after airdate," a contestant coordinator said.

He was just going to send the check to United Jewish Organizations of Williamsburg. They needed the money a lot more than he did.

Jeremy Wolf handed Brad a *Jeopardy!* tote bag, which contained a *Jeopardy!* baseball cap. He also gave Brad his suit bag.

"We need you out of here immediately," Jeremy said.

"OK," Brad said.

"I called you a cab back to the hotel, but you have to pay for it."

"Not a problem."

"You know where the exit is," said Jeremy.

Brad walked through the door. It clanged behind him and locked. They'd never let him into that room again. He wasn't going to go down in the annals of history; he was just a guy who appeared on *Jeopardy!* for a couple of days.

No one would ever call him champ again.

It was almost 5:00 p.m. The LA sun was, as usual, oppressively gorgeous. Brad put on his sunglasses. A cab pulled up to the steps. Brad told the driver to take him to an Irish bar on Pico.

For the next five days, Brad went on a Southern California bender worthy of Charles Bukowski and John Fante. On the sixth morning, when he woke up in his bed at the DoubleTree with a middle-aged truck-stop waitress from Tustin, he knew it was time to go. He flew back to New York, contacted a real estate broker, and sold his half block in Williamsburg to the highest bidder.

That was more than enough for him to move to Costa Rica, where he bought an estancia with excellent views of both the cloud forest and the Pacific Ocean. For the next six years, he did nothing but drink rum, smoke weed, surf, grow a beard, and bemoan his cursed fate. And that's where he sat, tanned and lonely, on the night before his fortieth birthday, listening to the monkeys howl in the jungle around him.

The longer Brad lived, the more alienated he became. He'd seen through the facade of existence, had cracked the secrets of time. Not like it mattered. Somehow he'd drifted through life the third time without making any actual friends. There was no one he could talk to about his situation after all. No one could relate. He had no love. He'd forgotten how to *feel*.

Everything was a lie.

He woke up in the womb.

FEDS INVESTIGATE CONTROVERSIAL INVESTOR
FBI TRANSCRIPT
June 15, 2007
Russo: FBI Special Agent David Russo
Bell: FBI Junior Special Agent Karen Bell
Cohen: Brad Cohen

Russo: State your name please, for the record.

Cohen: My name is Brad Cohen.

Russo: How old are you, Mr. Cohen?

Cohen: According to my doctor, I'm thirty-seven. But my doctor doesn't know shit.

Russo: So you're *not* thirty-seven?

Cohen: Depends on how you look at it.

Russo: How am I supposed to look at it?

Cohen: You can look at it any fucking way you want to, but it won't matter. Let's just say I'm older than you might think.

Bell: OK. Where do you live?

Cohen: I live in Manhattan. On the entire top floor in the tallest building in SoHo. Come on over. I'll mix you the most expensive drink you've had all year. Or I'll have my Filipino butler do it for me.

Russo: Do you have any other residences?

Cohen: [*Counting on fingers.*] Vermont, Malibu, and St. John in the Virgin Islands. Montana, maybe? Spain? I don't remember. I own property everywhere.

Bell: And you also have a yacht that you travel on frequently?

Cohen: Hell yes. It's the third-biggest yacht in North America.

Bell: How have you been able to afford these homes and this yacht?

Cohen: I could afford them because I bought them. With money that I fucking earned.

Russo: How exactly did you earn this money?

Cohen: Wouldn't you like to know?

Bell: That's the subject of this inquiry, Mr. Cohen. The government suspects—

Cohen: Suspects what? That I'm making a lot of money? Since when did the government fucking care about how people make their money? Are you going to tell me that I have weapons of mass destruction too? Your intelligence is bad.

Bell: Look, there are irregularities.

Cohen: Where?

Bell: Where what?

Cohen: Where are the irregularities? Tell me. I'll iron them out. I'll make them regular like my shit. I'll eat a gallon of fuckin' prunes.

Russo: It's a matter of cash flow really. There's—

Cohen: Too much cash? In all my lives, I've learned you can never have too much cash.

Bell: What do you mean, "all my lives"?

Cohen: What do *you* think I mean?

Bell: This is getting off track. We're trying to investigate—

Cohen: I know. You're trying to investigate why I have so much fucking money.

Russo: You could put it like that.

Cohen: I'll tell you.

Russo: Please do.

Cohen: Ever since I was a kid, in this timeline . . .

Bell: This timeline?

Cohen: [*Holds up finger.*] Just let me talk, you'll get used to it. All I could think about was money. How much there was, how much I didn't have, how I could get it. All of it. Or as much of it as the world would let me have. I wanted it all. All the fucking money.

Bell: You started making it young.

Cohen: As soon as I had any.

Bell: And when was that?

Cohen: I got $2,500 for my bar mitzvah.

Russo: What did you do with that money?

Cohen: I sank all of it into the stock market. A third went to Coleco, a third went to Telex, and a third went to Home Depot.

Russo: Why those stocks?

Cohen: Because I knew they were going to boom.

Russo: How? Did you have insider information?

Cohen: Sort of.

Russo: From where?

Cohen: From my fucking brain, OK? I know, always, which stocks are going to do well and which aren't.

Russo: How?

Cohen: Experience. Vast, endless, soul-sucking experience.

Bell: I don't understand.

Cohen: Neither do I. In any case, I sat on the stocks for about eighteen months, held the Home Depot—which was only going up—and traded in the other stocks. Half of that I plowed into Apple, and the other half I bet on the Chicago Bears to win the 1986 Super Bowl.

Russo: That couldn't have made you too much money. The Bears had pretty low odds that year.

Cohen: True enough. But I also correctly predicted the score and the MVP. Who does that, huh?

Russo: Not many people.

Cohen: The answer is, fucking no one. Except for me. I haven't made a bad bet in a hundred years. So I came out of that with about fifty grand, all of which I bet on the Mets to win the World Series in seven games against the Red Sox. I made that bet in April, when the odds were 250 to 1. So I really racked it up. I was 18 years old, or 138 years old—who knows the difference and who cares, I made a million dollars. And that was fucking nothing.

Russo: I have a note here that says your personal worth now is—

Cohen: About six billion dollars. Give or take a hundred million every time. It depends. Markets fluctuate. Real estate depreciates. And it's *really* going to depreciate around next year at this time. Sell off your assets if you can.

Bell: You're telling us that you made all this money—

Cohen: Legally, that's right, and no government cocksuckers are going to come in and take it away from me.

Russo: We're not from the IRS, Mr. Cohen.

Bell: But we could call them in if you like.

Cohen: I paid my taxes. Paid 'em all, except for the ones I didn't have to pay.

Russo: OK. Why don't you tell us what you did with this money?

Cohen: I bought shit.

Russo: What kind of shit?

Cohen: Real estate, watches, cars, TVs, a movie theater, a boat—I bought all the shit.

Russo: Drugs?

Cohen: I bought my first yacht. I parked it at a private dock off my property in the Hamptons. It was 1993. *Of course* there were fucking drugs. I did them all. Weed, amphetamines, Ecstasy, smack, crack, jack, fuckin' horse tranquilizers, acid, tequila mixed with absinthe, raw hash. It was *always* a party. A male prostitute injected liquid psilocybin into my dick. On my front lawn. During Sunday brunch.

Bell: Sounds fun.

Cohen: It *was* fun. One time I stuck a tennis ball up my ass, dipped my hand into a bag of cocaine, and jerked off until I screamed.

Bell: That doesn't sound like quite as much fun.

Cohen: My doubles partner was *not* happy.

Bell: Are you on drugs right now?

Cohen: I should be. You got any?

Bell: Wouldn't *you* like to know?

Russo: Agent Bell, stop flirting with the witness.

Cohen: She can't help it. All women are attracted to my unlimited wealth and bad-boy attitude.

Russo: Cut the shit, Cohen.

Bell: [*Clears throat.*] You mentioned some sexual acts earlier. Was there, um, a lot of sex in your life?

Russo: Bell, not relevant.

Bell: It might be.

Russo: [*Sighs.*] Fine.

Cohen: Was there sex? *Was there sex?* When you're rich and young and omniscient, there's always a shit-ton of sex. I've been fucking about three women and about one man a week for the last twenty years. Just the other night I had my dick in someone else's mouth while I was snorting coke off a stripper's tits and another stripper was shoving a dildo up my ass. It was fucking awesome.

Bell: You're lucky you're not dead.

Cohen: Is that what you're investigating me about? Fucking and doing drugs? Because I could name names. [*Cough cough.*] Robert Downey Jr., Cameron Diaz.

Russo: To be honest, Mr. Cohen, we don't care about any of that.

Cohen: There was this time when I put nipple clamps on my balls.

Bell: Go on.

Russo: No, Agent Bell. That's enough. What we want to know about is . . .

Cohen: You want to know why my clients make so much money.

Russo: Exactly.

Cohen: It always comes around to that. Everyone thinks I'm working a fucking scam.

Russo: You started Cohen Partners in 1995.

Cohen: Just in time for the first dot-com boom.

Russo: And what was Cohen Partners exactly?

Cohen: Well, at first we were an investment brokerage pretty exclusively. It was just five of us in a midtown office. The other four were only there because I couldn't make all the calls myself.

Russo: What calls?

Cohen: To clients.

Bell: And who were these clients?

Cohen: Anyone who wanted to take a ride on the Cohen carpet. We didn't care how much money they had. If they had faith in our advice, then we'd give it to them.

Bell: What advice is that?

Cohen: I would never advise a client to buy a stock that I wouldn't buy myself. In fact, if I haven't bought it, I won't promote it.

Russo: And what do you get in return for this advice?

Cohen: I get a fucking 10 percent commission if I sell it personally, and 3 percent of whatever my partners sell.

Bell: And your partners are fine with that?

Cohen: They don't complain. They do OK. Look, there is nothing wrong with taking commission when you're in business. It's a legitimate model. And my rates are fair, especially considering that I have never had a client ever who has lost money. Unless—

Bell: Unless what?

Cohen: Unless they don't listen to me.

Russo: And what happens if they don't listen to you?

Cohen: Then I have 'em whacked.

Bell: Excuse me?

Cohen: Naw, I'm kidding. If they don't listen to me, they don't make any money. Or they lose some. Either way, they learn their lesson. No one ignores me twice.

Bell: Or else you have 'em whacked, right? [*Winks.*]

Russo: Bell, he's a suspect in a federal investigation. You can't *wink* at him.

Bell: Fuck off, Russo, it's my *interrogation* technique.

Russo: It's not acceptable.

Bell: It's our dynamic. You're the uptight asshole and I'm the friendly one.

Russo: More like the party girl who's up for anything.

Bell: That remains to be seen. [*Winks again.*]

Russo: Stop it!

Cohen: I need some Jujubes to munch on while I watch this shit.

Russo: Bell will remain quiet while I ask the real questions. Right, Bell?

Bell: Hmph.

Russo: OK, Cohen. Basically we need to explain why everyone who ever does business with you ends up richer than before. It's highly irregular. It's more than that. It just doesn't happen.

Cohen: Shouldn't all business be like that? Since when was it against the law to make people wealthier?

Russo: Usually people who claim they can do that *are* breaking the law.

Cohen: Yeah, well, not me. There's no reason to fuck people over as long as I can get mine.

Russo: That's the American spirit.

Cohen: Fuck you.

Russo: So then there's the matter of the drug use.

Cohen: You got a warrant? Do you really want to fuck with my lawyers long-term?

Russo: No, but we were hoping you could rat out your dealers.

Cohen: [*Scratches head.*] OK.

Russo: Really?

Cohen: As long as you give me good witness protection. Preferably in the area around Vail. The global economy is about to collapse. Business will be slow. And I'm probably going to disappear in two and a half years anyway.

Bell: What do you mean, disappear?

Cohen: I'm not entirely sure. It's just something that happens to me.

Bell: [*Touching Cohen's hand.*] Aw. You look so *sad.*

Cohen: I am *vewy, vewy* sad.

Russo: Bell! Quit it!

Cohen: It's my fault. She can't resist my tragic countenance.

Bell: It's true.

Cohen: So, listen, if I give you information, I want something in return.

Russo: Depends.

Cohen: It's an easy thing. I need you to look up someone.

Russo: Who?

Cohen: Her name is . . . was . . . might still be . . .

Russo: What?

Cohen: Juliet Loveless. At least that was her name a long time
           ago.

Russo: OK.

Cohen: You might want to start in Chicago. She used to work,
           maybe, at the Art Institute. She might not still be there.
           She also might not exist at all. Or maybe she left the
           country. Or married someone else.

Bell: Someone *else*? Was she ever married to you?

Cohen: Yes. Then no. Then no again. And now, I guess not.

Bell: Who *is* she?

Cohen: I don't know who she is, or even *if* she is. But I can tell
           you who she *was*.

Bell: I'm listening. For as long as you need me to.

Russo: Goddammit.

Cohen: Once upon a time, there was a damn sexy witch . . .

JULIET

1997

Juliet Loveless worked thirty-three hours a week at the museum shop at the Art Institute of Chicago. She probably could have worked twenty-five hours—her portion of the rent on the place in Lincoln Square she shared with another woman (or, as they'd said in her postcolonial feminist theory graduate seminar, womyn) was only $400—but she took the extra shift so that she could pay for her correspondence course in herbal Chinese remedies. Every month a thick sheaf of poorly translated papers would arrive from Queens, and then she'd take the El down to Chinatown to find supplies and also eat soup dumplings. At night Juliet would make tinctures and then try them out on friends, with intermittent success.

That's really what she wanted to do full-time; she had a calling toward natural healing. But degrees were scarce, and paid clients even scarcer, especially in the Midwest. Meanwhile, the Art Institute job was fine. Juliet liked to stay busy, and there were always vast busloads of people and rafts of students pouring through the Art Institute's doors. Juliet found it hard to believe that there were still human beings alive who would purchase a framed poster of Monet's water lilies. But maybe she was just being cynical. Yes, Monet was overplayed, but so what? The haystacks were still beautiful, and people bought hundreds of postcards of them a day. She had a harder time rationalizing the Georgia O'Keeffe umbrellas, but at such moments she just rang up the credit card, smiled, and thought of ginseng. When you worked retail, it was best not to take the customer too seriously. Just give them the illusion of service and move them on along.

Usually the gift shop was packed full of the jangly earringed blue hairs of Kenilworth and beyond, but there were lulls, 3:00 p.m. Wednesdays, when Juliet could wander around the store straightening shelves and pretending to dust. She was doing that one afternoon when she looked up. Just a few feet in front of her was a guy, a really cute guy, or at least she thought he was cute. He was wearing a gray hoodie and had a bike helmet tucked under one arm. His brown hair flopped a little bit in front and looked messy, like it had been under that helmet for a while. He was skinny, which guys tended to be when they biked a lot. Juliet bet he had a nice butt, then immediately castigated herself for thinking about his butt, which was not what you were supposed to think, but it was out there now.

The guy was *staring* at her. She'd seen that look occasionally during sex, but that was usually temporary, or the guys were faking it. This one was *not* faking it. There was something in his eyes, something deep, something wise, something old. He looked at her like you'd regard a lover, not a stranger.

"Hi," he said.

"Hi, yourself," she said.

"It's really you."

"Of course it's really me," she said. "Who else would it be?"

"I can't believe it."

"Can't believe what?"

"That it's really you."

"Yeah, you said that. Are you going to stop being so weird and actually introduce yourself?"

"Oh shit," he said. "I'm sorry. That's right, you don't know."

"Don't know what?" Juliet said.

The guy extended his hand. "I'm Brad," he said.

She took it. "Juliet," she said.

"Brad Cohen."

"OK, Brad Cohen."

He looked at his feet and shuffled shyly.

"What is going *on*, dude?" Juliet said.

"I don't know how to say this," Brad said.

"Just say it."

"Well, I came to the Art Institute last week and I saw you through the gift-shop window. Since then I've been back every day to see if you were working, trying to get up the nerve to talk to you. And today I did."

"That's very creepy."

"I know," he said. "I hate to approach like this. But I didn't remember your phone number."

"*Remember* my phone number?"

"I mean, know. Know your phone number."

Juliet saw her supervisor regarding her a little suspiciously. A few oldster customers were starting to trickle in.

"Look," she said, "I have to work."

"I know, I know," he said. "I just want to spend one night with you, go out, get to know you. Have a *meal*. Something. Just talk. I'm not obsessed."

"You *sound* obsessed."

"I'm not. I just want to talk to you for a while."

"If you ask me out like a normal person, I will grant your wish. Otherwise, forget it."

Brad took a breath, seeming to gather his senses. "OK. Juliet. Will you go out with me tonight?"

"I have plans tonight. But I'm free tomorrow."

He looked very excited. "That's fine!" he said. "That's great! I will pick you up at seven."

"Make it seven thirty."

"Good."

He put a hand on her shoulder gently and gave her a low, sad, serious look. "See you tomorrow night, Juliet."

"Don't you want to know where I live?" she said.

"I already know where you live," he said.

"*What?*"

"Oh no," he said.

He looked alarmed, truly distressed. Juliet had never seen a person cycle through so many emotions in such a short period.

"Oh no, what?"

"I mean, I don't know where you live. North Side maybe?"

"Yes," she said flatly. "I live on the North Side. Doesn't everybody?"

"Not everybody," he said. "I live on the South Side."

"Fair enough," she said. "There's a Polish bakery just off Lawrence on Damen near my place. Pick me up in front there."

"I will," he said. "I won't be late."

"I bet you won't," Juliet said.

That night, Juliet met her roommate Margaret for their weekly drinks at the Hopleaf. Beers were expensive there. Some pints ran three dollars and fifty cents or four bucks. But they were good beers, and the place was a short bus ride away.

"It was weird the way he looked at me," Juliet said. "It was like he *knew* me."

"Guys try that move sometimes," said Margaret.

"But this wasn't fake," she said. "Not like he was trying to look into my soul. He just knew everything. It was really intense."

"Well, you've got to follow through," Margaret said. "You could use a little intensity in your life."

"I guess."

"That accountant you've been dating is really boring."

"I found his pot stash," Juliet said. "And then he tried to lie and say it wasn't his."

"Did he even *offer* you any?"

"No," said Juliet. "That was the worst part."

"The bastard."

"I don't even like to smoke weed. It makes me sleepy. But it's a really interesting medicine."

"Medicine," Margaret said flatly.

"Yeah, it contains all kinds of chemical compounds. There's the THC, of course. That's the chemical that makes you high. But they're doing all kinds of research in Israel and Europe. There's another chemical called CBC that has been shown to reduce seizures."

"Huh."

"And it has a lot of other uses as well. It can help reduce pain and stimulate the appetite. There's even this one strain that they've developed in Amsterdam that, if you ingest enough of it—usually in liquid form—it can create these incredible lucid dream states that seem to go on forever."

"Like hallucinations?"

"More intense than that. More realistic. Almost like deep psychic medicine. Your brain reshuffles your life while you sleep and you don't even know it's happening exactly. It's almost as though your brain can live in several realities concurrently. They say that time gets so compressed, it almost becomes meaningless."

"Sounds heavy," said Margaret.

"It's in the early stages of research," Juliet said. "They're doing clinical trials in Holland."

She took a sip of beer. "Man," she said. "It's *amazing* what herbs can do. I would love to do work like that."

"You could research on me," Margaret said. "Unofficial."

"Nah," said Juliet, "you're not fucked up enough. Nine times out of ten, you'd still end up being the music editor of *New City*."

"True enough," said Margaret, who had devoted her professional life to the arduous task of listening to amazing live music six nights a week.

"Maybe," Margaret said, "you could research it on this guy who came to visit you at work. Sounds like he could use some help unpacking his brain."

"I don't know anything about him," Juliet said, "except that he might be stalking me. Or that he's some kind of psychic."

"Juliet, if there's anyone I know who could handle dating an actual psychic, it's you."

That was true enough.

———

Juliet waited outside the Polish bakery. The pastries in the window glowed unnaturally, greens and pinks, some kind of hideous marzipan that seemed to sit in the window for weeks at a time. You could probably play street hockey with most of the pastries. The bakery didn't ever seem to have many clients. It was usually just a half-dozen beefy men sitting around playing checkers and drinking coffee. Any time you got more than a mile away from a heavy yuppie district, half the storefronts became either covers for the Mob or for Democratic party regulars, which were often the same thing.

But it was so much local color as far as Juliet was concerned; they never bothered her. And no one else ever bothered her either when she was in front of the store. That was for sure. She had other problems, like the freaking cold. Her scarf wrapped around her neck three times. She tucked her chin into her chest. She'd grown up in Arizona, where it only got this cold once a year and then only if you went up into the mountains. But here she was, standing on a street corner on the North Side in October, and she could practically feel the ice crystals forming in her nostrils.

A man was walking up the street toward her. He wore a long peacoat and a tall hat with a thick, furry brim, vaguely Slavic in style, not out of place at all in this neighborhood. His breath came out in thick puffs, seeming to surround his head like smoke clouds. There was a lot of it too, making it look like he was emerging from some sort of self-generated mist.

He got closer, and Juliet could see that it was Brad.

"Hello there," he said.

"Hello," she said. "I thought you said you were picking me up."

"Here I am!"

"In a car."

"Oh," he said. "I don't have a car. I could get one if you want."

"You can just get a car?"

"Sure," he said. "It's not like they're a rare commodity."

That was true enough. Most of Juliet's friends didn't have cars. *She* didn't have one herself. But it would have been nice tonight.

"That's OK, we can take the El," she said. "Or walk. Or whatever. But I'm going to be cold."

"Of course you're going to be cold," he said. "It's Chicago."

"Where are we going anyway?"

"Not far. I was thinking we could grab some Peruvian food," he said, "and then the Handsome Family is playing at Schubas."

"That's one of my favorite types of food," Juliet said. "And one of my favorite bands."

"I know," Brad said.

"How do you know?"

"I guessed."

"Then why didn't you say 'I guessed'?"

Juliet would soon have a lot of conversations like this with Brad. It sounded like a fun night, though. Decent taste in food and music can blot out the crazy. At least for a while.

———

Brad let Juliet do the ordering. She got them a *ceviche mixto* with white corn, a traditional *causa*, which is kind of a potato and avocado casserole, and a big order of *lomo saltado*.

"All we need is some coca tea and we'll be set," Juliet said.

"That can be arranged," Brad said.

"I've already got it at home," she said shyly. "I'm an herbalist."

"I know," Brad said.

"How do you know?"

"I mean, you seem like an herbalist type."

"What type?"

"Kind of like a sexy witch."

Juliet blushed and found herself getting warm.

"Ain't nothing sexier than a sexy witch," Brad said.

"You're weird," Juliet said.

"You don't know an eighth of it," Brad said.

The food started to arrive. They went at it eagerly.

"Man," she said, "Peruvian food is my *favorite*."

"I know," he said.

Stop knowing things about me, she thought. *Can't you just say, "That's cool"?*

But he didn't, because he knew everything. When they got to the bar, he already knew that she liked mournful country ballads and watered-down Leinenkugel, preferably together. They talked about reading, and he already knew that she hated pretty much all books written by someone named "John." They talked about politics, and he already knew that the health care system was a conspiracy of idiots designed to actually keep people unhealthy. He understood. In fact, he said, he'd written an article once for the *New Century* about that topic.

"When did you write for the *New Century*?" she asked.

"I don't remember exactly," he said. "A while ago."

"How can you not *remember*?"

"It's complicated."

"I guess so!"

"But I can tell you that things are going to get way worse with health care. It's all going to come to a boil in about 2009."

"How do you know that?"

"I know."

He did. He knew everything. It was ridiculous. Between Handsome Family sets, he talked about the history of the dulcimer, which Rennie had played with such mournful beauty. He didn't just say he was *familiar* with the dulcimer, or with dulcimer music, which would have been unusual enough; he knew the *history* of the instrument. Juliet couldn't even decide if she liked this quality.

"You sound like a guy who's obsessed with collecting records," she said.

"I won't touch records," he said. "Or CDs either. Almost all music is going to be digital fifteen years from now and people will mostly listen to it on their phones."

"Oh, come on!"

"Trust me," Brad said. "In any case, I like to see things live. It's like a little piece of history that I can remember forever. I have a lot of history. In fact, I studied it for years."

"You've done a lot for a guy who's—how old are you? Twenty-seven? Twenty-eight?"

"I have lived for hundreds of years," Brad said.

"You don't look a day over a hundred," she said, but his face was actually pretty grim.

"My body is young," he said, "but my mind is old. I am Connor MacLeod of the Clan MacLeod. I was born in 1518 in the village of Glenfinnan on the shores of Loch Shiel. And I am immortal."

Well, it wasn't the *usual* date. Juliet wasn't sure what to make of this guy and his seemingly sincere *Highlander* references, but he had plenty of interests. At one point she said to Brad, "You should be on a quiz show, like *Jeopardy!*"

"Oh, I've been on *Jeopardy!*" he said ruefully.

"Really?" she said. "When did that happen?"

"Soon?" he said. "Never. I don't know."

"Did you win?"

"Yes."

"That's amazing! How much?"

"Fifty grand, give or take. I gave it to charity."

"You did *what*?"

"Look, could we talk about something else?"

They did, and it was about a quarter past two when Juliet rolled into her apartment, feeling surprisingly warm even though the wind outside was nipping like a thousand airborne Chihuahuas. You could even say she glowed. Margaret was on the couch, smoking a fatty.

"How's it going?" Juliet asked.

"Wesley Willis spat on me, and then I went to the Bucket with Cynthia Plastercaster."

"The usual then."

"Pretty much."

Margaret took a drag and handed the joint to Juliet, who accepted it gladly. She needed to relax.

"What about *you*?" Margaret asked. "How was your night with the sad prophet?"

"It was kind of amazing," Juliet said. "He wrote for a magazine and was on a game show."

"He sounds like a fucking dork."

"I don't know," Juliet said, her eyes glimmering a little. "He has an old soul."

"Barf. What does he do for a living?"

"I don't know, but he paid for everything, including my cab fare home."

"Huh," Margaret said. "The last guy I went out with asked to borrow money so he could pay his rent."

"He kissed me too," Juliet said.

"What are you, Audrey Hepburn? Was it a *French* kiss?"

"Yes," Juliet said.

It had been a good one too. At the bar after the show, Brad just leaned in, gently touched her chin, and tilted it upward. He was so gentle about the whole thing. His eyes almost looked scared, like he was about to lose something very important. The kiss was gentle and lingering, and amazingly private considering that they were at a bar whose population largely consisted of drunken options traders.

"I have searched for you across the fields of time," he said to Juliet, and he didn't appear to be saying it ironically.

"What is he, the Highlander?" Margaret said. "Can there be only one?"

"Mock if you want, but I'm going to see him again."

"I'm sure you are."

"If you'd take out the trash soon, I'd appreciate it. Brad might be coming over, and the kitchen smells like dead fish."

"It's not my turn."

"It is. I did it last week."

"I disagree."

"I would appreciate your support."

"And you have it. But I am not going to be your butler while you live out some sort of weird Wicker Park romance novel."

Juliet huffed. "Fine," she said, and went off to her room, which was just off the kitchen and which did in fact stink of garbage. Someone would definitely have to take it out. She and Margaret had reached this impasse before. In reality they weren't very good roommates.

She laid down on her single futon, stared up at the dream catcher hanging over her bed, and put a Kate Bush CD on, volume low. She took care not to brush her toes against the white-hot steam radiator.

"Brad Cohen," she sighed. "You are weird."

———

They dated three times a week, sometimes four or five. It wasn't like she had a lot of other stuff going on. Brad called every other day, and he always had good ideas. They did all the fun Chicago stuff. There was a show at the Upright Citizens Brigade, highlighted by a goofy Lucille Ball–like blonde who Brad insisted was going to be very big news someday, and also a sketch thing called Dratch & Fey at Second City. Brad said, "I would buy stock in Tina Fey if I could." They saw Mary Zimmerman's production of *The Arabian Nights* at the Steppenwolf. There was a Bulls game followed by a gorge at Mr. Beef on Orleans, and a Sunday evening old-man jazz jam at the Velvet Lounge, just off Roosevelt. He took her down to Maxwell Street and advised her to take photos because it would all be torn down soon. They went to a Bob Wills Hoot Night at the Hideout, where Jon Langford, Robbie Fulks, Kelly Hogan, and Freakwater played, and stayed out late doing shots at the Matchbox, "the world's smallest bar." There was tequila at Weeds and pints at the Old Town Ale House. They rode trains and buses and cabs all over the city, wrapping their scarves tight against the bitter winds, and occasionally even going down to the lake to watch the forming ice slush against the shore.

In some ways it was the most fun Juliet had ever had. She'd never known a man—or a woman for that matter—who knew as much or had as many different interests as Brad did. He was always on time, always polite, and didn't seem excessively interested in putting the sex moves on her. In fact, she would have slept with him on the third date and told him so, but he just kissed her gently and said, "Not yet. I want to get reacquainted better."

And that's where it got confusing. Sometimes he said things that simply didn't make sense to her, like "Nineteen ninety-six is going to be a good year again," or "Al Gore is going to win an Oscar." He would refer to things that had happened in the past as though they were going to happen in the future, and to things that seemed to be in the future as though they were going to happen in the past. And sometimes in the present his eyes would glaze, as though he didn't quite know where he was. When they went to movies, he seemed really bored, as though he'd seen everything before. One night at this Italian place that was fast becoming one of their favorites, she caught him staring at his hands, muttering to himself, "So young. Always so young."

Brad was all mystery all the time. She didn't know where he lived or where—even if—he'd gone to college. He said, "I grew up in Hyde Park. Several times." But other than that, he didn't discuss his past or his childhood. If he had a job, he didn't talk about it. He always seemed to be free to do anything at any time.

One night he picked her up at her house in a BMW 3 Series. She didn't know he had a car or even a driver's license. He'd told her to dress nicely, so she'd put on a skirt and blouse. But he was wearing a tuxedo.

"If I'd known we were going to prom," she said, "I'd have rented a dress."

"We're not going to prom," he said. "We're going to Charlie Trotter's."

In that era, Trotter's was far and away the nicest restaurant in town, and you never got out for less than $200 a person. Juliet had been once. Her father had taken her as a college graduation present.

"I can't afford that," she said.

"I'm paying," said Brad.

"*You* can't afford that," she said.

"Sure I can."

Who was this guy?

"How?"

"I invested my bar mitzvah money in Apple stock," he said. "And I put ten thousand dollars on Villanova to beat Georgetown. Before the season started."

She had no idea what that meant.

"Basically," he said, "I'm rich."

It didn't matter to her, but it was good to know.

Charlie Trotter's was as stuffy as Juliet remembered—guys folding napkins in her lap and terrines with their own special forks, and soup served in a golden bowl. They ate seven courses and didn't talk much.

"You're awfully quiet," she said.

"Well," he said, "I know everything about you. And there's not much to know about me."

She was still hungry when it was all over.

The valet pulled up Brad's BMW and held the door open for her.

"You seem unimpressed," he said.

"It was fun," she said politely, "but not really my style."

He smacked himself in the head. "Of course not!" he said. "I am so stupid!" Brad turned his face to the sky and shouted, "I am fortune's fool!"

That was weird. And kind of cute.

"No you're not!" said Juliet.

"I'm not?" he snuffled.

"Of course not," she said. "Tomorrow night we'll go get some real food. If you're free."

"I'm always free," he said.

He rang her doorbell at 7:00 p.m. He was wearing jeans and an old gray sweatshirt and looked like he hadn't slept much.

"Did you park the beemer downstairs?" she asked.

"Oh no," he said. "I sold that today. We're taking the bus."

They rode the number 11 for fifteen minutes down Lincoln Avenue. It was sleeting, and the bus's heating wasn't working very well. Maybe Brad had overcompensated slightly.

As they neared Wellington, Brad pulled the wire. The bus dinged and pulled up to the curb with a loud puff. Brad got off first. He offered Juliet his hand. She walked down the step. He didn't let go. In fact, he was gripping a little too hard.

The place was cute inside, South American down-home, lacquered wood and native garments and photo murals of old Cartagena. A collection of Cumbia music was playing over the PA. You sat at benches at long tables, and it wasn't very crowded. Juliet and Brad had their own table in the corner.

"How'd you find out about this place?" she said.

"It just opened two weeks ago," said Brad. "I've known about it for a long time."

"How . . . ?" she said, but then stopped herself. This guy was a living temporal cryptogram.

Juliet let Brad order this time. He seemed to know what he liked, and what he liked was usually pretty good, or at least it was authentic. This time, though, it was authentic and incredibly delicious. They had the *matrimonio*, "marriage" in Spanish, a mixed grill of steak and shrimp served with taro root and a side of homemade *chimichurri*. Brad also ordered a *sopa de mariscos*, which was full of fish and herbs.

They were deep into their second bottle of wine when Juliet exclaimed, "This food makes me so happy!"

She saw Brad's eyes get teary.

"I hoped it would," he said. "I *knew* it would."

"I'd rather eat here than anywhere in the world," she said.

Most of that second bottle of wine had been hers, and she was appreciably drunk at this point.

Brad reached across the table and took her hands. "I love you, Juliet," he said. "I always have, all these years."

"I love you too," she said.

But at the same time, she thought, *Wait, what am I saying? I don't love him. I don't even know where he lives.* She regretted it, but regretted it even more when he started sobbing softly at the table.

"Oh God," he said. "It's happening. It's really, really happening."

She had to distract him.

"What have they got for dessert?" she asked.

They took a cab home. He pawed at her desperately, kissing her neck, sucking on her ear. She was dizzy and drunk and sort of returned his affections, all the while thinking that she smelt like a cork that had been left on the counter too long.

The apartment smelt worse than that. She and Margaret had been feuding about the garbage for weeks. Brad gagged when they walked in the door.

"Don't worry," Brad said. "When you live with me, I'll always take out the garbage. It's my job."

"Where do you live?" she asked.

He touched her face tenderly. "I have a beautiful place. For us," he said. "Only for us."

Margaret wasn't home. They stumbled to the couch. He kissed her more deeply than she wanted, like a starving man who's happened onto a meal. She kissed back, though, and even helped him unhook her bra. They were both drunk, she a little more than he, but there was no resistance on either part.

"I love you, Juliet," he said. "Love love love you."

He climbed on top of her and started to rub. She felt him against her thigh, stiff as a pole.

"Oh God oh God oh God oh God," he said.

"Mmm?" she said.

"At last at last," he said.

She looked up. Brad's face contorted weirdly, like a shriveled grape.

"*Mmmmmmmmmm,*" he said.

She felt him hitch against her thigh. There were two rhythmic thrusts, and then a growing wetness. His cock deflated like an improperly tied balloon animal.

"Oh no!" he said.

He sat up. A viscous stain spread across his khakis, making a shape like some weird forgotten continent, an Atlantis of premature jizz.

"I'm so sorry," Brad said.

Juliet sat up and stroked his hair. "It's OK," she said. "It happens."

He started to sob again. "I just wanted it to be perfect."

"We can do it again in a couple of hours."

He was really blubbering now. "I miss our daughters," he said.

"Our *what*?"

"There are two of them, and they're so kind and sweet and funny. One of them has no attention span, and the other one can sit for hours and makes art and she throws up all the time."

"We don't have daughters, Brad."

He grabbed her by the shoulders.

"But we *will*, Juliet," he said. "That's what the future is about."

Juliet stood up. She walked over to the built-in china cabinet and pulled open the top drawer, where Margaret kept the weed box. There was a pipe with a little nug left in. She lit it and took a drag.

"You need to leave now," she said.

He looked at her with mournful, pathetic eyes. "But—"

"You need to leave, and you need to forget my phone number and where I live, and you are never to call me or see me again or I will get a restraining order against you."

"This isn't how it's supposed to go," he said.

"There's something wrong with you," Juliet said. "I feel bad, because you're obviously suffering, but I was not put on this planet to fix your problems."

"You used to be," he said.

"There you go again!" she said. "Stop talking like you know me or knew me, or whatever. You know *nothing*."

Brad stood up, looking sad.

"Please," he said. "Don't leave me. I won't do it again."

She stood with her hands on her hips, lips pursed.

"I know that look," he said. "You'll let me come back."

"*Go!*" she said.

He walked toward the door, head down, and turned to look at her.

"You poisoned me!" he shouted. "You and your witch brew!"

"What?" she said.

"Why?" he said. "Why did you destroy my liiiiiiiife?"

"You are scaring me."

"Why can't it be like it was?" he said.

"I don't know what you're talking about."

"Yes, you do," he said. "I know that somewhere in there, you do."

She'd never seen a look so searching or lost.

"You have to go," she said, "now. Or I will call the cops."

"See you," he said, and he went into the night.

Juliet went to the door, double-bolted it, sat down on the couch, and had a cry—deep, long, satisfying, and a little drunken.

A half hour later, there was a rattling at the door.

"*I said go away!*" Juliet cried.

"Dude," said Margaret through the door. "Let me in. I dropped my keys in the toilet at the Empty Bottle."

Juliet unlatched it. Margaret came in, cold looking and red-eyed.

"Is he out there?"

"Who?"

"Brad?"

"I didn't see anyone."

"He could be hiding in the alley or something."

"I don't like the guy, but that doesn't seem like his style. Is it over?"

"It's over," Juliet said.

"Finally," said Margaret.

In fact, Brad had walked over to Irving Park Road, and he was in the process of walking down Irving Park to the lake, which was going to take him a while, but he didn't care. He knew there wouldn't be anyone around. The snow had started to fall, heavy and mean and wet. Chicago had gone into hibernation, a mode that Brad had experienced way too many times, hundreds even, maybe less, maybe more. He didn't know any longer, and he didn't care.

Brad crossed Lake Shore Drive at the light, and then he crossed the empty bike path and then a set of basketball courts and walked down a freezing, lonely beach of sand hiding under snow, and then out to the pier, a long walk strewn with pebbles and fish bones. Lake Michigan lapped up against the moldy concrete—relentless, cruel, and eternal. He crossed two decades of graffiti, stood at the end of the pier, and tossed his hat into the churning, icy waters. Then he removed his scarf and his gloves and his jacket and his sweater, his long underwear, his shoes, his socks, his jeans, and finally his boxer briefs, flinging them one after another into the lake.

The weather battered him, but he didn't care. He'd taken every shock the world could offer, and he'd borne them all. And still he felt the pain, the confusion, the misunderstanding, all the horrors of being alive, of being forced into the same body, for the same years, over and over again. He stood there against the gray-black sky—naked, freezing, and alone.

Brad turned his head to the sky and raised his hands. *"Why me?"* he shouted.

It was all probably a little much. He didn't even have an audience. But it had been a rough couple hundred years.

"Why me? Why me? Why me?"

But the universe had no answer for old Brad Cohen.

———

Within a year Juliet Loveless had stumbled into an opportunity to travel to Holland to study with the Dutch doctors who were doing groundbreaking research into the medicinal properties of cannabis. A six-week fellowship became a job, and that led to a master's degree and a better job and a PhD from Leiden University, and by 2006 Juliet was one of the leading researchers in the burgeoning field of herbal medicine, a genuine doctor in a world that needed them terribly. She married a Dutch man, relatively late, had one miscarriage, and then at age thirty-nine had a daughter. But she was living in a place that actually had social services, so she kept her career going and by the year 2014 was spending the autumn and winter in Tucson, Arizona, working with Dr. Andrew Weil, and the rest of the year in Holland. Her husband worked for her; her daughter went where she went. All told, her life was a lot better without Brad Cohen's emotional wreckage holding her down.

Still, from time to time Juliet thought of that weird, haunting, passionate boy who'd tried so unsuccessfully to seduce her in Chicago in the mid-'90s, and wondered what happened to him. She didn't wonder too hard, but he was in her mind like any lover stays, at least partially, forever. One slow night in Tucson, she looked him up on Facebook and Twitter and the other social bits of the web she used. It wasn't easy. Brad Cohen was a common enough name. It was a real rabbit hole, though. Maybe he was one of those guys who lived off the grid on a concrete slab in Nevada. But she didn't remember him as that sturdy or brave. There seemed to be no digital evidence of him at all. She couldn't even find an online death record.

In 2015, Brad Cohen didn't exist.

THE MAN WHO KNOWS EVERYTHING
Chicago Reader
April 11, 1998

By Neal Pollack
Staff Writer

Every day for the last three years, a gaunt, sad-looking man named Brad Cohen has been riding the El, mostly the Red Line but occasionally the Brown and Blue, telling people the future. Not everyone listens to him, but a surprising number of people do. He's never rude, he's usually clean, and there's often something persuasive in his eyes. Even though Cohen looks biologically to be somewhere between twenty-five and thirty-five years old, he claims to actually be somewhere between four hundred and five hundred, possibly even more. "I'm not quite sure," he says. "At some point you just lose track of time."

One morning last November, I met Cohen on the Belmont El platform, which is one of his preferred spots because it's where a lot of lines converge. He says he gets some of his best work done on the Evanston Express. He was wearing an expensive-looking navy peacoat and a pair of nice sunglasses, and could easily have been mistaken for an upscale guy headed to work in the Loop. This, as I later learned, is one of Brad Cohen's most mysterious qualities. Other times when I met him—and we've spent a lot of time together in the last few months—he looked as though he'd spent several nights in a row behind a Dumpster. His attention tends to wander and doesn't always focus on normal human needs, like dressing properly or bathing or living indoors.

He shook my hand with a businessman's force.

"What a pleasure," he said. "I've wanted to meet you for a long time."

"Why?" I said, since no one ever wants to meet me.

"I'm a completist," he said.

That was a strange thing to say, but I soon came to learn that Brad Cohen says a lot of strange things. His mind seems to work on several simultaneous tracks, not all of them comprehensible, even to him. The Ravenswood train arrived, and we got on, headed downtown. Slowly as usual, the train rumbled away.

"I tend to prefer going toward the Loop," Cohen said without prompting. "When you travel out into the neighborhoods, people are heading home, and they don't really want to hear the truth. They're more ready for distraction when they're on the way to work or whatever. Are you ready to watch me?"

"Sure," I said.

"OK," he said, and he stood up, cupping his hands to his mouth.

"Attention, ladies and gentlemen," he said. "I'm sorry to bother you during your commute. Some of you may be familiar with me, or maybe not, so let me introduce myself. My name is Brad Cohen, and I'm the Man Who Knows Everything. Now, I'm not asking you for money. I'm just asking you for the opportunity to let me tell you the future. It's a gift that I have, and I want to share it with the public for free. Ask me anything."

There was silence in the train car. People looked at their books or at their shoes. We were getting close to Fullerton, and soon we'd go underground.

"Keep in mind," Cohen said, "that I don't have psychic powers. Unless you're famous—in which case you're probably not riding the El . . ."

That elicited some chuckles. As Cohen told me later, "I've lived a lot of years in Chicago. I know they like that regular-guy appeal." On the train that day, he continued, "Or are going to be famous, in which case you probably don't mind hearing that's the case—I can't predict your individual futures. But I *can* tell you everything that's going to happen in *general*. Anything at all. And I'm always right, a hundred percent of the time. I highly recommend that you try me."

The train pulled up at Fullerton. As it pulled away, a guy from the back of the car shouted out, "Are the Cubs ever going to win the World Series?"

"I think you know the answer to that," Brad said. "Two thousand three and 2004 are going to be particularly heartbreaking."

"What about the Sox?" the guy asked. There was a bit of booing on the train, pretty common on the North Side.

"Please don't shoot the messenger," Brad said to much laughter. "But yes. The White Sox are going to win the World Series in 2005."

This elicited even more laughter.

"And they're going to beat the Astros."

Now Brad had the train car in the palm of his hand.

"Who's gonna be president after Clinton?" someone asked.

"George Bush, the governor of Texas."

"Bullshit!" a man exclaimed.

"It's true. He's going to steal the election from Al Gore, and the reason he's going to be able to do that is because Ralph Nader is going to enter the race and take votes from Gore's left flank."

"What about after Bush?"

"Well, that's where it gets interesting. He's here in Chicago right now. It's Barack Obama. He just got elected to the State Senate."

"That guy is black!" said a black guy.

"I know that," Cohen said. "I can vouch for it personally."

I make a note to myself, "Call Barack Obama." About a week later, I do that, and I get Obama on the phone at his office in Springfield. I ask Obama if he's ever heard of anyone named Brad Cohen. At first, Obama says no, but as I'm just about to hang up, he says, "You know, now that you mention it, there was a guy named Cohen who showed up at my community-service office back in

'93. He kept telling me that I was going to be president someday, which is completely absurd, and that he wanted to volunteer for me. Well, we could always use volunteers back then, so I accepted his offer. He was really good for a while, did whatever I asked, but after about a month, he just started standing in the corner and muttering to himself, so we had to ask him to leave because he was scaring people away."

"So are you going to be president someday?" I asked.

"I am committed to serving the people of the state of Illinois," said young Mr. Obama.

Back on the El, Cohen fielded a couple more questions. At Division he said to me, "Let's get off here. I'm thirsty."

On the street, he said to me, "It's always the same questions over and over. 'Who's going to win the World Series?' 'Who's going to be president?' Like that's all that matters. No one has any damn imagination. I could tell them that the earth is going to fly off its axis and hurtle into the sun and all they'd care about is whether or not the Bears are going to the Super Bowl."

"Well, is it?" I asked.

"Is what what?" he said.

"Is the earth going to hurtle into the sun?"

"Not as of 2010 it's not," he said.

We went to the Old Town Ale House and ordered pints. Brad insisted on paying.

"I have so much money, I can't spend it all," he said.

The mystery was thickening.

"There's a portrait of me on the wall here, as part of the mural," Cohen said.

"Is that right?" I said. "I thought the mural was painted in the '70s."

"It was," he said. "I used to come here with my dad sometimes. In the mural I'm a kid."

We picked up our beers and walked over to the wall, where local hacks, poets, improvisers, novelists, and other bohemian luminaries had been immortalized in hues of brown, yellow, and orange, which looked even worse than they once had, because of twenty-five years of tobacco stains. It's a memorial to the town's pantheon of forgotten weirdos. Brad walked over to a far corner.

"See," he said. "I'm right . . . here." He pointed at the lower right corner.

"That's not you," I said, "unless you're a young Del Close."

Cohen looked at the mural. "Huh," he said. "Ask the bartender."

We walked over to the bar together. Brad ordered another round of beers.

"Hey," he said to the bartender, a woman about as old as Alderman Ed Vrdolyak but only about half as well preserved, "can you tell me what happened to the painting of the kid on the lower right corner of the mural over there?"

"There ain't never was no kid, sweetheart," she said.

"No, I'm sure there was. It was me. Don't you remember a kid used to come in here with Don Cohen?"

"I don't remember nothin'," she said.

"Huh," he said.

He turned to me. "That must have been from a different time-line," he said.

"A different timeline?"

"I get them confused."

For the Man Who Knows Everything, he certainly didn't seem to know himself very well.

———

Cohen grew up in Hyde Park, the only son of a University of Chicago economics professor and a social worker. At least that's what he told me. Unlike some of his other claims, though, this one was easy to check. I called Don Cohen at his office at the U of C. He got back to me a couple of hours later.

"I was just confirming that Brad is your son," I said.

"Why?" said Don Cohen. "Is he in trouble again?"

"Not that I know of."

"Good. There was this time a few weeks ago where he was claiming to be the alderman from Albany Park and he chained himself to the desk of the ward office. Another time he got arrested at Superdawg because he was screaming at the manager to show him the title for the place. He said he was the owner."

There was a sigh on the other end of the phone.

"It's a lot of trouble being Brad's father," Don Cohen said.

I arranged to meet Don and Rose Cohen at their condo in Hyde Park, the place where Brad grew up and where they still live. They offered me oolong tea imported from China and cookies from their favorite *panadería*. Clearly, Brad had grown up in an intellectual household, almost a bohemian one.

Don and Rose's apartment was as dusty and book filled as you might imagine, with fraying rugs and framed Harold Washington campaign posters and ads for shows at the Checkerboard Lounge on the wall. There were issues of the *Nation*, *Mother Jones*, *Harper's*, and the *Baffler* on the coffee table, and a nice display of native Guatemalan art. Rose Cohen told me she'd done quite a lot of pro bono work with refugees from the Guatemalan civil war.

"I even took Brad with me to Antigua a few years ago," she said. "It was kind of shocking how bored he seemed, like he'd been there a dozen times before. He even knew the name of the woman who owned the hacienda we stayed at."

"He's always been like that," Don Cohen said. "He would never do his schoolwork but knew all the answers. He could read at a college level when he was in kindergarten but rarely found anything that could hold his attention. We tried to put him in Hebrew school, but he *already knew Hebrew*. How was that even possible?"

"Did you have him evaluated?" I ask.

"Of course we did!" Rose said. "We took him to Dr. Bruno Bettelheim, for God's sake. The doctor said Brad was of above-average intelligence but nothing exceptional and showed no signs of schizophrenia or other form of mental illness. He didn't have attention-deficit disorder and didn't register on the autism scale. We went to the Mayo Clinic. We went everywhere. *Nothing was wrong with him.*"

"But everything was wrong with him, obviously," Don said.

"Days would pass by and he wouldn't come out of his room. Also, after 1983 he was rich."

"What do you mean, rich?" I asked.

"He had a lot of money. He invested half his bar mitzvah money in Apple stock and then picked the Tigers to win the 1984 World Series . . . before the season even started! That was fifty grand right there. He invested half of that in Microsoft and then took the other half to pick the next World Series winner. It just went on like that. By the time he was eighteen, he could have afforded to send himself to Harvard thirty times."

"But he didn't go to college," Rose said. "He said he didn't need to. Or want to. He said he'd been before multiple times."

"I don't understand," I said.

Rose blew into a tissue.

"Brad had . . . has . . . *memories.*"

"Like past lives?"

"Not really," she said. "More like memories of *this* life, of things that have already happened. He has so many of them that he gets confused. And you want to know the strangest thing?"

"What's that?"

"I *believe* him."

"He can be very persuasive," Don said. "In 1985 he said to me, 'Steven Spielberg is going to make a movie about the Holocaust, and it's going to win the Oscar.' At the time it sounded like the stupidest thing I'd ever heard, but he was correct, and about so many things, over and over again."

"It must have been hard having a kid like that," I said.

"You have no idea," Don said.

Rose smacked him on the arm. "He never gave us any trouble," she said. "Not really. He didn't mouth off and had decent manners and was never impolite. It was the inconsistency that made it hard. Things would go OK for a week or two, even a month, and then he'd just wander. One time I took him to Jewel because I had to pick up some groceries, and when I turned around, he was gone. I got totally frantic. I looked around for a while, and it really seemed like he had disappeared for good this time. He always said to me, 'Mom, someday I'm just going to vanish, so don't get attached.' I had no idea what that meant, but maybe this was it, right? As it turned out, he was just standing in the corner between the juice and milk refrigerators, walking in place with his head against the cooler. It was like, what do they call it when a computer or a video game stalls out?"

"It crashes?" I said.

"Right, it was like he was having some sort of crash. I touched his shoulder. He turned around. His eyes looked so lost and scared. And then he completely snapped out of it and said, 'Oh, hi, Mom. How are you?' He had no idea where he was."

"How old was he when this happened?" I said. "Eight? Nine?"

"No, he was twenty," said Rose. "He moved out of the house soon after that, and we've barely seen him since then. He won't call for months at a time."

"And then a few weeks ago," Don said, "I came home from the office, and Brad was sitting in the kitchen. 'What's for dinner?' he asked. We went out for Ethiopian food and he fell asleep at the table."

Rose put her hand on my arm. "Honestly, you can tell us," she said. "Is he doing OK?"

I wasn't sure how to answer her.

"He's fine," I said.

———

I met with Brad Cohen a half-dozen times over the next month, and every time his story just grew stranger. He claimed to have been a senior editor at the *New Century* magazine and a multiple-time champion on the game show *Jeopardy!*, to have been Lou Reed's personal assistant in 1990, and to have worked as part of the maintenance crew for New Zealand's America's Cup team. According to Cohen, he's lived in Caracas, Cincinnati, Ann Arbor, Jerusalem, Paris, Wheeling in West Virginia, both East and West Berlin, and, for a brief period when he was "investing in oil and gas exploration," in the Russian town of Smolensk. "Those are just the ones I can remember right now," he said to me. "There are dozens more." He says he's climbed Mount McKinley, Mount Fuji, and Mount Kilimanjaro, and attempted to swim the English Channel once but had to stop when he got a puncture in his wetsuit. One summer, apparently, was spent biking across Spain, and another hitchhiking around Scandinavia. He says there is no place he hasn't been, no drug he hasn't tried, and nothing he hasn't done. He speaks of everything with authority and in incredible detail. And yet there's absolutely no evidence that any of those claims are true.

I worked as a junior reporter myself at the *New Century* once, in the summer of 1991, so I made a few calls over there. No one had any memory or knowledge of Brad Cohen, except for Jacob Jaffe, the paper's editor and guiding spirit.

"Have you ever heard of Brad Cohen?" I asked him on the phone.

"Well, of course," Jaffe said. "Everyone in this business knows at least *one* Brad Cohen."

"Fair enough," I said, "but I'm talking about a specific one."

I went on to describe Cohen and his background in detail.

"Come to think of it," Jaffe said, "there was one morning about five years ago, during the buildup to the Gulf War. I came in early because we had a guy in Iraq who was faxing us dispatches. No one was there except for our receptionist, who for some reason likes to use the shower in my office. I let her because—I don't know, let's not talk about that. In any case, there was a kid sitting in the bullpen, typing away."

"Who was that kid?" I asked.

"He might have been your Brad Cohen," Jaffe said. "He said to me, 'I'll have my briefs done by lunchtime,' and I said, 'I didn't order any briefs, and I don't think you work for me.' He looked at me so sadly and said, 'Of course I do, Jacob. I'm your best guy; you told me so yourself. And any time you want me to take over the magazine, I'm ready.' He looked so sad and lost, I almost let him stay, but you know how competitive those bullpen slots are."

"I do," I said.

"So I told him he had to leave. He started to cry. He said, 'But I belong here!' Then I threatened to call security, so he picked up and walked away, shoulders slumped. After he was gone, I looked at the briefs he was working on, and you know what was funny?"

"What?" I said.

"They were excellent. So prescient."

A few days later, I got Barbara Stevens, the lead contestant coordinator for the game show *Jeopardy!* on the phone. I asked her if there'd ever been a player named Brad Cohen on the show.

"I would have to check," she said. "We cycle through a lot of people every season. And most of them vanish without a trace."

So I described Cohen in some detail to her.

"You know, it's strange you should say that," she said, "because I remember now a couple of years ago this young man showed up at the studio one morning with all the other contestants. He'd gotten on the bus at the hotel, and he knew exactly where to go. He even knew all of our names. In fact, he was so persuasive that he got all the way to the greenroom and was filling out a form before we realized he wasn't on the roster."

"So what happened?" I asked.

"Well, of course we told him he had to leave. Getting on the show requires passing a rigid series of tests. And, you know, there's security screening. He said, 'But today is my taping. I'm supposed to win two games and then I lose the third, and I'll donate the money to charity, and I'll be out of your hair forever.' I said, 'I'm sorry, sweetie, it doesn't work that way.' And then he said the strangest thing."

"What?"

"He said, 'I must be in the wrong timeline,' and he picked up his suitcase and headed for the door. I offered to call him a cab, but he just walked out the door. 'I know the way,' he said. It was pretty disturbing. He seemed so lost. But we had to let the incident go. We had a show to tape."

Every interview I just got more confused and had to visit Cohen again. Finally, for the first time, I went to his home. He lives in a small three-room apartment a block from the Jarvis Avenue El, just above Don's Coffee Club, a vintage-themed café, where Cohen can be found many evenings nursing a pot of tea and a huge piece of store-bought chocolate cake. He has a regular table near the back, which he always gets to use because he's also the building's landlord. In fact, he bought the entire block of buildings on Jarvis in 1989, when real estate values in Rogers Park were at their lowest. Cohen's mother says he's always had an uncanny knack for predicting property values. Brad doesn't charge Don rent and only asks him to cover utilities.

"He doesn't ever talk to anybody in here," says Don Selle, the café's sole proprietor and sole employee. "He just sits there for hours, staring into space, asking me to play Louis Prima and Keely

Smith duets. Which is fine, because the rest of the customers hate it, and I want to drive them away because I don't feel like working."

Cohen's apartment is just upstairs from the Coffee Club. He had me walk up the back stairs rather than the front entry. I could hear "(I've Got a Gal in) Kalamazoo" playing as I went up the stairs, which were wet from a recent rain. Cohen's rear apartment door was unlocked. I opened it and went inside. It was dark. There appeared to be no furniture. Then I spotted a single futon mattress on the floor and a paper chest of drawers. The apartment smelled like dirty clothes, and also like there hadn't been a window opened in there for years.

"Hello?" I said.

There was a rustling in a far corner. I looked over. A shape was moving around. I flicked the switch on the wall next to me. Brad Cohen was squatting in the corner, looking at the wall. When the light (from an unshaded bulb) flooded the room, Cohen turned his neck toward me. He hissed like a cornered animal.

"What do *you* want?" he said.

"Um, you told me to come over and talk to you tonight," I said.

"Did I?" Cohen said.

"Yes."

"Who *are* you?"

I told him. He squatted there, looking confused.

Finally, he said, "Oh, yes, you're doing a feature story on my . . . *situation.*"

"What exactly *is* your situation?" I asked.

"I think you know," he said.

We both agreed that the apartment was no place for a conversation. There was nowhere to sit, and it smelled like an abattoir.

"I don't need much," Cohen admitted.

So we went down to the Coffee Club, where Selle served us reluctantly, even though there was only one other customer in the place, who kept asking Selle if he could open up his laptop, and Selle kept saying, "No electronics! Books only!"

Cohen told me that this was his dream establishment. "Don's the only person who wants to be here less than I do," he said.

When I'd met up with him twenty minutes earlier, he'd acted about as normally as a caged human in a *Planet of the Apes* movie. Brad ordered us two slices of chocolate cake, which I saw Don cutting. He'd clearly bought them at Jewel earlier in the day. We also got two pots of tea. Finally, I broached the topic.

"I don't understand who you are," I said.

Cohen sighed. "Tell me about it," he said. "I'm just myself over and over again."

"You're clearly about my age, but you seem . . . older."

"I'm so much older," he said. "I don't even know how old."

"But you're *not*!" I said.

"Look, you seem frustrated," he said, "and I understand if you don't want to pursue this anymore. I don't care either way. In one timeline the guys from Kartemquin Films, the ones who made *Hoop Dreams*, started making a whole documentary about me. But they quit because they couldn't figure out the story. But I will tell you this. I'm not a con man. And I am *not* crazy. Or maybe I am a little crazy, because this situation has driven me crazy. So let's put it a different way. I'm not making anything up. I have lived many lifetimes, or at least partial lifetimes. It could be forty or fifty or sixty, or as many as seventy-five times. The count eludes me. Regardless, I have gone through puberty more than any man should. I have been to many colleges. I can unfortunately remember most episodes of *Barnaby Jones* by heart. One time I got my dad to let me see the Rolling Stones during the *Tattoo You* tour, the one with the tongue on the T-shirt, but other than that it was only after the *Undercover* album, which was *not* a good show. I saw Oingo Boingo and Adam Ant in 1982, and I saw Nirvana play with

Kurt Cobain at the Metro *sixteen* different times. There were a lot of James Brown shows mixed in there too."

This was all very discursive, but he kept on going. "I worked on an oil rig in the Gulf of Mexico and as an account executive for an oil company in the Strait of Hormuz. I saw the genocide happen in Rwanda, at least until they evacuated me. I saw the Berlin Wall fall in person three times in a row. I went surfing in Belize the day before a hurricane. I ran for Congress and lost. And another time I ran for Congress and won, but I resigned before I took office because I didn't want to work with Newt Gingrich."

"It all sounds fake," I said. "All of it."

"But it's all real. Ask the women."

"What women?" I said.

"Oh, there have been women," he said. "Some men from time to time for variety, but mostly women. Imagine being single for more than a thousand years."

"I haven't particularly enjoyed being single for *twenty-seven* years," I said.

"Consider yourself lucky."

I asked him if he knew how to get in touch with any of these women.

"Most of them I don't remember," Cohen said. "But there are a few."

He named a few that he could remember but kept coming back to a young woman named Juliet Loveless, who, he says, as best as he knows, works at the gift shop of the Art Institute of Chicago.

"I was married to her once a long time ago," he said. "We had two daughters. But I haven't spoken to her in hundreds of years."

"What do you mean, hundreds of years?" I said.

"I mean that once a very long time ago, or what feels like a long time ago to me, I was a washed-up screenwriter in Hollywood, married to Juliet. We had two beautiful daughters, named Claire and Cori, and we lived in a shitty old house on top of a hill. The night before my fortieth birthday, I had a breakdown. Juliet made me some kind of herbal potion and I fell asleep. I've been trapped in an infinite time loop ever since, and I can't figure out whether or not she did this to me. OK?"

"That sounds like a great premise for a novel," I said.

"Go ahead and write it," Cohen said. "See if I fucking care."

There were some other things I was curious about.

"You say you know everything that's going to happen?" I ask.

"I do to a point," he said. "Not about everyone. But everything in general."

"Do you know what's going to happen to me?"

"Wait," he said. "What's your name again?"

I told him.

"Oh, yeah, I know that dude. You're going to be a newspaper reporter in Chicago."

"I already am that."

"Then you're going to get a little boost when you start writing for an Internet magazine called *McSweeney's*. Dave Eggers, a writer who'll be more famous by his thirtieth birthday than you'll ever be in your lifetime, will publish your first book, and that'll get your career going for real. There's some nonsense with a punk-rock band and a novel to go along with it, which will flop."

"The novel or the band?" I said.

"Both."

"Naturally."

"Then you're going to publish a memoir about being a 'cool' dad. Last thing I remember, you're going to get into yoga."

"That all sounds very unlikely," I said.

"I know what I know," Cohen said.

"So what happens after that?" I ask.

"It all gets a little hazy after 2010," Cohen said. "That's the cut-off point. It always is. I disappear."

"What do you mean, you disappear?"

"I mean that I stop living on the night of my fortieth birthday. I go to bed and wake up in my mother's womb, and then I get born and it's 1970 again. I have to live my life again, in order. It's like *Groundhog Day* but four decades long, and I have to wear diapers for the first two years."

"Damn," I said.

Cohen turned to Don, the proprietor of the joint, and said, "Hey, Don, this cake is really good tonight!"

"It's the same shit it always is," Don said.

A couple of days later, I went to the gift shop at the Art Institute of Chicago. Juliet Loveless was working behind the counter, a pretty, confident young woman in a flowing skirt.

"Do you know someone named Brad Cohen?" I asked.

"I don't *think* so," she said. "Why?"

"He claims to know you."

"Huh," she said. "How?"

"He says you were married once."

Juliet laughed. "That's hilarious," she said. "I've never been married."

"So you haven't had any contact with him at all?"

I described him to her.

"Well," she said.

Here we went again.

"About a year ago, there was this guy who came into the shop. He was carrying flowers. And he gave them to me. I'd never seen him before. He said it was our one-year anniversary. I said, 'I'm sorry, I don't know you,' and he said, 'It's me, Juliet. It's Brad, your husband.' My manager called security, but he was gone before they could get here."

"And you haven't seen him since then?"

"You know, I could have sworn I saw him peeking in the window once a couple of months ago, but it was only briefly. When I looked again, he was gone."

"He hasn't tried to visit you at your home?"

"Now you're creeping me out," she said.

"I'm sorry," I said. "I don't mean to. But has he?"

"Maybe he's tried," she said. "I was living in an apartment in Lincoln Square until a few months ago, but I moved in with my boyfriend. Should I be worried?"

"I definitely think you should *not* be worried."

"Who is this guy?"

"I don't know," I said.

I really didn't, and I still don't. Brad Cohen grew up in Hyde Park, got rich in the most improbable way imaginable, and then has spent the next decade bumbling around Chicago and occasionally elsewhere, never really sure where he is and what he's doing. As far as can be discerned, he never got an education to speak of. And yet he seems to know everything. He's one of our city's weirdest mysteries.

A few weeks later I was riding the El downtown, and he got on board at Belmont.

"Attention, ladies and gentlemen," he said. "I'm sorry to bother you during your commute. Some of you may be familiar with me, or maybe not, so let me introduce myself. My name is Brad Cohen, and I'm the Man Who Knows Everything. Now, I'm not asking you for money. I'm just asking you for the opportunity to let me tell you the future. It's a gift that I have, and I want to share it with the public for free. Ask me anything."

"Hey, Brad," I said.

He looked at me with incomprehension.

"Do I know you?" he said.

"Yes," I said, "we've been hanging out on and off for months."

"I don't think so," he said. "Not in this timeline."

What other timeline could there be? I wondered, but I decided not to press the issue. Better to let Brad Cohen work it out for himself.

"Now then," he said to the train car. "Who wants to know the future? You? Me? Anyone? No?"

He turned to me and opened his arms wide.

"Shabba-doo!" he said.

THE NINETY-NINTH SERIES

NINTH SERIES

MYSORE, INDIA

1993

The little portable alarm clock went off at 4:00 a.m. Brad didn't care. He'd gone to bed at eight, like he always did, before the sun had gone down. Those were the only hours when it was cool enough to sleep here anyway. He knew, because he'd been here for six months. This round. There had been other runs at Mysore in previous timelines—a few months here, a few weeks there, the odd year or two when he didn't have anything else going. It was hot. Then it was pleasant for about three weeks. And then it rained. Brad never noticed anymore.

Popping his lower back into place, Brad got off the floor, where he slept on a straw mat. He had few possessions: his alarm clock, a canteen, a teakettle, a backpack, a couple of shirts and changes of underwear, a deeply thumbed copy of *The Yoga Sutras of Patanjali*—a book he was thoroughly sick of—and his passport. Brad kept most of his money, of which he had a lot as always, in a reliable bank in Bangalore. Every month it wired a certain amount to the *shala*, plus a little extra. For the time being, at least until Madonna showed up in a few months and started preaching Ashtanga yoga to the West, Brad was still propping up the place. He was glad to do it; yoga kept his muscles taut and his mind relatively clear. It was the only thing left keeping him from running into the sea, a raging madman.

His room had no adornments save a fraying photo of Sri Krishnamacharya, who had emerged from a cave in Tibet nearly a hundred years previous with a system that would save us all. There was also a rusty mirror. Brad looked at himself; his hair was long and matted, his beard not much more kempt. He weighed maybe 150 pounds, probably less.

Brad pulled on a pair of loose-fitting pants. They were made of hemp. He'd bought them at a thrift store in Berkeley, which sold such things. His upper body looked skeletal, like he'd been on a hunger strike. But he just didn't care anymore. He knew exactly what he needed to eat to survive. About one week a month he spent writhing in pain from amoebic dysentery. The rest of the time he subsisted mostly on a diet of dal and rice, one huge helping around noon. A couple times a week, he'd treat himself to a mango *lassi* in the heat of the afternoon. Sometimes he could still enjoy the sweet essence of things. Rarely.

He went downstairs to the courtyard and pumped well water into his canteen. Then it was back to his room, where he boiled it for tea. He kept a jar of that, strong-smelling and black, usually Darjeeling, on a wooden shelf in his room. He drank greedily, splashing the remaining water on his face. He took two showers a week at the public bathhouse, and he also got a hot-oil massage. A lot of the other students lived in proper hotels, or even houses, and had amenities—maybe not as many as they would have had at home but still plenty, way more than most people in India had. Brad could have afforded every luxury, but he'd had every luxury he could ever want in his lifetime, which at this point was getting very close to four thousand years long. He knew very well that human beings essentially needed nothing to survive, especially if they were only going to be around for forty years, the young and healthy years.

After his tea it was time for Brad to head to the *shala*, which was two blocks away. They didn't open the doors until four thirty, but Brad liked to be there at the start. His practice took a long time. Ten years from now, he would *have* to be there early if he wanted a spot. He'd made that mistake in previous timelines, finding himself nose to butt with dozens of type-A Ashtanga trendoids from all over the globe. But in 1993 it was just him, a few hippies, and a couple of decimated rich ladies turned seekers. And none of them were as far down the path as he was.

He was there before Guruji's bleary-eyed grandson unlocked the doors.

"Hello, Brad," said the boy. Brad nodded at him ascetically, walked into the room, which was really just a room, almost totally unadorned save the usual portrait of Krishnamacharya and a couple of Ganesha figurines. The walls and floors were dark, cool clay. It was not a special place or a sacred place. In Sanskrit, the word *shala* means "barn." It was a deadly serious practice, this yoga, at least the way the people who'd adopted it went about their business, but Guruji refused to give them a fancy setting for it.

Brad went inside. He was the first one there. No one else would show up for at least an hour. There had been an emaciated-looking Swedish woman who'd beat him to the mat a few times in April, but she'd long ago gone back to Stockholm, as Brad knew she would, because he'd run across her in his travels before. He also knew she'd be back next year but would pop a hamstring halfway through third series and quit in frustration. He had no idea if she'd be back again. He wasn't God. At least not yet. That probably wasn't where this was all going.

He unraveled his mat, the same one he'd slept on the previous night. Even though he washed it at least once a week, it still smelled like a landfill of shoes. By the time things got going in the *shala*, five hours of yoga sweat from at least a dozen people, it wouldn't stand out at all. Even now it barely registered.

Brad sat on the mat, legs crossed. Guruji wouldn't show up until at least 5:00 a.m. Not like Brad needed him for the opening poses anyway, which he'd been doing for, what now, 150 years? Two hundred? Brad didn't remember and didn't care. Guruji was doing his own practice at this hour, preparing himself for the rigors of guiding a select group of paying Westerners toward something that bridged the gap between penitence and enlightenment. For now it was Brad, alone, in a dark and quiet room. He could feel his breath move from the top of his head, his crown chakra, down through his body, through the central channel, the *sushumna nadi*, and out through his *mula* at the base of his spine. Or maybe it was all just in his lungs. Regardless, his mind was focused, his breath regular, his gaze steady, his body taut and ready. Brad chanted silently to himself, the opening prayer of the Ashtanga system, which Krishnamacharya himself had brought down from that Tibetan mountain cave.

Brad rose. He stood at the top of his mat, inhaled, and raised his arms above his head. It was time to begin.

———

Somewhere along the line there—was it his eighty-fifth incarnation? His eighty-seventh?—Brad Cohen started practicing yoga. His time period, 1970 to 2010, was actually perfect to take up the practice, coinciding with a boom in the West. He liked it immediately. After exhausting any possible mode of human experience that he wanted to try and then spending hundreds of years essentially ranting in the wilderness, it was the only thing he found that could calm his mind down at all. A couple of hundred years and several births later, he hooked into the Ashtanga practice.

That was the best bet for Brad, because a real Ashtanga practice chewed up at least two hours every morning and then left him feeling so wrung out and exhausted that he could barely even worry about the fact that he was trapped in an infinite time loop, doomed to wander throughout a limited period in human history.

Some afternoons he was so exhausted that he could barely lift his head off his chest. It took everything he had just to gulp down a glass of water. And the practice never got any easier.

Ashtanga is divided into six series, and the practitioner isn't allowed by his teacher to move on to the next series until he's mastered the present one. Each one is more difficult than the next. Even if you master the sixth series—which almost no one ever does—you still have to do the first one sometimes. The process doesn't end.

But Brad had mastered the sixth series. In fact, he'd arrived in Mysore almost all the way there, which led Guruji to say, "Have I taught you before?" The answer was, "Yes, but then my life repeated itself," but instead Brad said, "No, I've just been practicing on my own." Within two months he was fully conversant in the sixth series, at which point he'd asked Guruji what he should do.

"Do you know God?" Guruji had asked.

"Of course not," Brad said.

"Then you must practice more. Practice, practice, practice, and all is coming."

Brad was sick of hearing that. But regardless he kept at it in hopes that somehow he could see his way clear of this mess through yoga. He definitely felt calmer and clearer than he had in centuries. It wasn't enough. He wanted out, but he couldn't figure out the path.

By the time his *guruji*, Shri K. Pattabhi Jois, arrived in the *shala* a little after 5:00 a.m., Brad was already almost finished with the opening sequence, a group of poses that he'd done countless times, so often that they almost seemed innate, like breathing. Today was Tuesday, so that meant Brad needed to do the second series, what he called the "easy poses," a series of inversions that included a half-dozen versions of headstand, meant to counteract the effects of the heavy, grounding first series that he'd plodded his way through the day before.

Pattabhi Jois, squat and bald and in his early sixties, walked around the room carefully in his T-shirt and shorts, looking like a yoga version of Mr. Clean. He was always in the mix, making adjustments, pressing down on people's backs, threading their limbs through seemingly impossible gaps, but he had nothing for Brad Cohen. Brad had done the practice so many times. He knew all its intricacies.

By 8:00 a.m. he was done, and he lay on his mat asleep, as wrung out as a kitchen towel, while later-arriving students grunted and gyrated around him. It was a long *savasana*. Brad had nothing better to do. Finally, he snorted awake, sat up, and chanted silently to himself. Then he sat even more silently, his hands on his knees, and absorbed the sounds and smells around him, his thoughts and emotions all integrated into one long channel of universal awareness. And yet still the thought occurred to him: *In fifteen years I will disappear. And then I'm going to have to start all over.*

Brad stood, rolled up his mat, and headed for the door. Much to his surprise, Pattabhi Jois came up to him and touched his arm. He almost never did that and hadn't since Brad had shocked him three lifetimes ago by finishing the fourth series in its entirety on his first try.

"You are done with the practice," he said.

"I am?" Brad said.

"I cannot teach you any more."

"I don't agree."

"Come to my house tonight," said Guruji. "For dinner. At five o'clock. We must discuss."

"Discuss what?" Brad said.

But Guruji had already moved on and was cramming an overeager German into *kurmasana*. Brad could hear the joints crackle and was glad he didn't have to do it anymore. He had his invitation, maybe to enlightenment.

For the rest of the day, Brad wandered in a daze, as he often did. He drank his water, ate his dal, took a nap through the heat of the day, paused for a moment at a knife-sharpening spot to watch an artisan grind his blades, and then went to the bathhouse for his shower and rubdown. What great insight awaited him at Guruji's house? He went back to his room, put on a clean shirt—the one with buttons—his hemp pants, and a pair of sandals. It was as close as he could get to formal wear.

It didn't really matter. Pattabhi Jois lived next door to the *shala*, in a modest five-room house. His wife let Brad in. Guruji was sitting in an easy chair, watching TV. All of India was enraptured by a lavish adaptation of the Mahabharata, being presented in something like five hundred parts over a period of two years. Pattabhi Jois was no exception. He didn't speak to Brad until the episode was over.

"This is the greatest story," he said. "Next year, the Ramayana. Do you like?"

"Of course," Brad said. He'd seen the whole production two or three lifetimes ago.

"We must talk," said Guruji. "About your practice."

Guruji was a deeply intelligent man, though his education had been almost entirely yogic, learned at the feet of the great Krishnamacharya in the palace of the maharaja of Mysore in the 1930s and 1940s. His English comprehension was good, but the speaking sometimes came out a little pidgin.

"OK," Brad said.

"You have no more to learn from me," said Jois. "How is that possible?"

"You won't believe it," Brad said.

"It is OK," said Jois. "You can tell."

Pattabhi Jois wasn't going to understand. No one did.

Brad sighed.

"Guruji," he said, "I have lived many lifetimes."

"We all have," said Guruji. "It is the cycle of karma."

"No, I have lived the same lifetime over and over many times, never ending, always repeating."

"Birth and rebirth, it is all sensation," said Jois. "It is all yoga. We must work to focus the gaze and trust the breath. Practice removes *samskara*, eliminates suffering."

"I get all that. I have done that work."

"It is true," said Guruji. "A true yoga practice requires many lifetimes. Practice, practice, practice, and all is coming."

"Not for me."

"Even for you."

"But I'm caught in an infinite time loop."

"What is that?"

"Some sort of weird temporal anomaly that causes me to repeat my entire life over and over again."

"That is an illusion," Jois said. "The ultimate *samskara*."

"I wish that were true," Brad said. "But I have memories, deep memories, of almost a hundred lifetimes. I am always born in Chicago, and then I do a bunch of stuff after that."

"This is life," Guruji said. "This is normal. It is all practice."

"For what?"

"For death. For meeting God."

"But I don't die," said Brad.

"Everyone dies."

"Not me. I don't even get old. I always disappear on the day before my fortieth birthday," Brad said.

Guruji took a sip of tea.

"This," he said, "is *not* normal."

"What should I do, Guruji?" Brad said.

Pattabhi Jois pondered this for a moment.

"Maybe you should go see Mr. Iyengar," he said.

———

Brad Cohen wandered through the world, hungry and alone, and ended up on the West Coast, where the climate was decent and he had plenty of company in the land of the lost. This was nothing new in itself. He'd done it dozens of times before. He begged for food but had plenty of money. Then he felt guilty about that, so he gave half of his money to an organization for homeless people in San Francisco. It didn't matter. Everything he did felt old and useless.

When he got tired of city living, he went to a storage locker he kept in Oakland, pulled out some camping equipment, and took the bus north up to Sequoia or Yosemite or Tahoe, sometimes all the way to Summit County, Colorado, and he'd rent a site for a month, with just enough food to get through the day. For hours he'd sit under a tree and meditate. That's what the Buddha had done. He'd sat and focused his mind, and then he realized the impermanence of all things. But the impermanence of Brad's situation felt in itself permanent. Maybe that was the point.

Brad went to a campsite in the far reaches of Sequoia National Park. It was April, just the beginning of the season. He'd taken a bus, then hitched to the park entrance, and hiked in—not too far, maybe three miles. There was only one other campsite, where an Audi SUV backed up to an iron grille. A middle-aged couple and three kids, two boys and a girl, were playing in the stream, walking around, looking calm and happy, together, untroubled.

He tried to remember a time when he'd been happy himself. His memories kept going back to that crummy house he'd lived in with his wife and daughters, up there in the scrubby hills, way northeast of LA. But had he been happy? From what he could recall, that life had brought him nothing but sadness and dissatisfaction. They weren't in that house now, and neither was he. His daughters didn't exist. They hadn't for hundreds, thousands of years. Yet he still longed to see them. Or at least longed to long to see them.

Brad sat. He wasn't sure for how long. It could have been minutes or hours or days. He barely saw the difference between day and night anymore. He felt thirst, recognized it as such, and then went along, still sitting. It was cold—he registered cold—and then it was warm. There was numbness. Maybe he shifted position. He wasn't sure, just as he wasn't sure how old he was, what day it was, what year it was, or who he was in any way. Everything had broken down.

All his demons, everything accumulated over the centuries, roared before him, trying to bring him into their drama, to upset to worry, to force a reaction. But he just let them do their dance. This is what he'd been seeking, that visceral knowledge that his problems were temporary, even when it seemed like they weren't. Everything flowed past like debris carried in a river after the storm, being washed out into the churning sea.

And then he remembered. It wasn't much of a memory, but it was something. He and Juliet had taken the girls up to the Griffith Observatory, but it had been closed for cleaning, so they'd driven a little farther up the road, up near the Hollywood sign, and somehow there'd been no traffic, human or otherwise. It had just rained the day before, so the sky was blue and crisp, and the air was free of lawnmower noise. They'd parked the Prius and walked down the path a couple hundred yards maybe, about as far as the girls could go without whining. He had one attached to each hip, and he was holding Juliet's hand, and she was smiling at him. Also, Brad was just a little bit stoned. At that moment the world had been perfect, his mind free and untroubled.

It could always be like that, he realized. It *was* always like that. No matter what, you could access that perfection. It just took a little serendipity, and in Brad's case nearly two thousand years of near-relentless whining. The world is a shit dump, but it's all we have, so we might as well treat our time and the people we encounter in it with a little tender feeling.

Brad opened his eyes. It was midday. What day, he couldn't tell. But the air smelled fresh and clean and cool. A girl maybe seven years old was standing in front of him, holding a little snack bag of Fritos.

"Hi," she said.

"Hi," he said.

"My daddy said you look hungry."

Brad thought about that.

"I *am* hungry," he said.

"Do you want these?"

She extended the hand with the Frito bag.

"I do," he said.

He tore open the bag, and the Fritos were down his gullet within seconds. She gave him a plastic bottle of water.

"Do you want this too?" she said.

It was gone equally as fast.

"If you want to come have dinner with us, you can," she said.

Brad smiled.

"Dinner sounds nice," he said.

That night Brad Cohen fell asleep outside while staring at the stars.

The next morning, he woke up in the womb.

But this time, rather than trying to force anything onto his life, to think too hard, he just lived it as it was meant to be lived, in order. He experienced all the anxieties and bouts of loneliness and pettiness that he'd always been meant to experience, moments of doubt and frustration and stupidity. He made some good choices and made some bad choices and didn't try to stop any of them. Most of all, he spent his bar mitzvah money on comic books, just like he had the first time, thereby robbing himself of the chance to enjoy a lifetime of wealth. Brad just existed exactly as he had the first time through, without judgment, participating actively but not stopping to fret about results. It was his life, and he lived it the best he could. He met Juliet and allowed the relationship to unfold without comment, judgment, or attachment. Just his life, happening in real time, and it was beautiful.

Even when he made what he'd previously considered his fatal life decision, to chuck his career and move to Hollywood on a whim, he didn't try to stop himself. It didn't occur to him. He needed to let the disaster unfold. Nothing was going to stop him from spending a year as a staff writer on *Battlecats*.

Then came the day before his fortieth birthday, and he suffered through the humiliations at Fox, where a massive windstorm had destroyed his pitch. He got too stoned to drive, but he drove anyway. He and Juliet went out to The Sideshow and spent too much on a meal they couldn't afford. Then he went home and broke down sobbing in front of the girls, and he had such a terrible headache, and Juliet gave him some sort of potion to drink, and he went to bed happy.

Brad woke up . . .

AT LAST, THE FINAL CHAPTER

. . . feeling awful inside and out. He knew that sensation in his head and his stomach: too much wine, too much food, and too much weed. It was familiar, but not. He opened his eyes. There it was—that big, cracked yellow stain on his bedroom ceiling. And the door looked all black and scratched from the dog rubbing against it way too many times. The draft came in from the window, which was never sealed all the way. It was always pretty much the same temperature inside as it was out. He opened his mouth and closed it. The usual thin layer of grit was in the air.

Wait. The *usual* thin layer of grit? Where was he?

He opened his mouth, but his voice felt raspy. There was a glass of water by his nightstand. He took a sip. It felt not too fresh, but not deeply stale either.

"Juliet!" he called out.

His wife opened the door five seconds later.

"Yeeeeeees?" she said.

"It's you!" he said.

"Of course it's me," she said. "It's always me."

"How long was I asleep?" he said.

"Ten hours," she said. "Maybe eleven. The usual."

"But—"

"How do you feel?" she said, smiling kindly.

Like shit, he thought, but then he thought again.

"I feel amazing!" he said. "When is it?"

"What do you mean, when is it?"

"What day is it?"

"It's Wednesday."

"Which Wednesday?"

"The Wednesday of your fortieth birthday."

"My what?"

"Your fortieth birthday."

"Really?"

"Really."

"I'm forty?"

"Yes."

Brad burst out of bed, feeling as fresh and excited as a twelve-year-old on vacation getaway day.

"I made it!" he said.

He threw his arms around his wife, who looked at him bemusedly.

"Ah ha ha!" he said.

Brad ran out of the room and through the living room, where his daughters were eating bacon and strawberries and watching *SpongeBob*.

"Hello, my beautiful ladies!" he said.

"Happy birthday, Daddy," said the little one.

He picked her up and kissed her head twenty times.

"Stop it, Daddy," Cori said. "You're making my hair wet."

Then he did it to Claire, though she made him stop after five kisses.

"I love you guys," he said. "Love love triple looooooooove."

"That's enough," said Claire.

"Wait," he said. "Why aren't you in school?"

"There's no school today, Daddy."

"Why not?"

Juliet came in the room.

"It's a furlough day."

"Goddamn fucking public schools," Brad said. "Where does the tax money go anyway? How are we supposed to get anything done around the house if . . ."

His family was looking at him. Brad caught himself. No. He was not going to let this bother him. Not today. Not anymore.

He ran to the front door, flung it open, tore down the driveway, and stood in the street.

"*I am alive!*" he shouted.

Linda, the babysitter, was walking a dog, not hers, right past as he said that.

"You're also not wearing any pants," she said.

Brad looked down.

"Oh," he said. "Sorry."

"It's OK," she said. "I've done it many times. Sometimes on purpose."

"I'm alive, Linda!" he said.

"I can see that."

From the doorway, Juliet said, "Brad. Come inside."

Brad turned around.

"Alison is on the phone," said Juliet.

"Alison who?" he said.

"Your manager."

My manager. Brad hadn't thought about her for thousands of years.

He took a look at the outside of their rental house, at the rotting wood around the eaves and the foundation, at the shabby little weed trees in the front yard, at the uneven, cracked driveway. He walked up the sidewalk, nearly breaking his toes as usual on the concrete steps, which had been poured on the cheap, probably by a drunk or a team of drunks.

"This place is a shithole," Brad said.

"I know," Juliet said.

"But I love it!" he said. "And I love you!"

"Well, that's nice to hear, honey," she said as she kissed him on the cheek.

Brad went inside. His cell phone was sitting on the kitchen table.

"Hello?" he said.

"Happy birthday!" said Alison.

"You remembered," said Brad.

"No, your wife told me."

"Oh."

"I'd really love to meet her sometime, Brad."

"You have met her. Many times."

"Oh, really?"

"Yes."

"I apologize. I take a lot of pills. So, listen, *we* need to meet. Are you free today?"

"I don't remember," Brad said.

"Can you check?"

"Sure."

Brad looked around the room, trying to orient himself. He had a work space somewhere in the house. Where was it? Oh yeah. It was in the garage. Basically a hole. A man-hole full of pot and Dodgers memorabilia. It could have been worse. Brad wondered how the Dodgers were going to do this season. Then he realized he didn't know. What a relief not to know something.

"Brad?"

"Yeah."

"Can you check?"

"Sure."

"Are you crying?"

"Yes."

"Cut it out."

"Right."

Brad went into what passed for his office, checked his date book, and found it wanting for commitments. All he had written down, for the next six weeks, was "write," and then not every day. Also, he had a dentist appointment in about three weeks.

"I think I can fit you in," he said.

"OK," she said. "Meet me at the Starbucks in Burbank, the one next to Bob's Big Boy, in an hour and a half. Can you do that?"

"Sure," Brad said.

"Don't be stoned."

"I won't. Am I in trouble?"

"I wouldn't be meeting with you in person if you were in trouble," she said.

Brad got off the phone. Juliet was waiting for him.

"What's up?" she said.

"I have a meeting," he said. "With my manager."

"When?"

"Soon. I have to take a shower."

He looked at his wife.

"I am very much in love with you right now," he said.

"Ewwwww," said the girls.

"Go take a shower, weirdo," said Juliet.

The shower was as disgusting as always, cracked and slimy and misshapen. The water tasted hard and metallic, almost dirty. Brad could see twenty feet down into the earth through the drain. It felt so good.

He shaved, looking at himself in the cracked, spotty mirror, put on a clean shirt, kissed his family more than they wanted to be kissed, and headed out in the Prius he couldn't afford. It still had four blips of gas. He could drive back and forth to Burbank all day and still have enough in the tank for the weekend. Life was glorious.

Alison was waiting for him at the Starbucks when he arrived. At least he thought it was Alison. He had a hard time remembering what she looked like. But she waved at him, so it must have been her.

They hugged.

"How *are* you?" he said sincerely.

"Ugh," she said. "I fucked my ex-husband last night. The morning was *not* pretty when the pool boy showed up."

"I see," he said.

"And I had to give my poodle Klonopin because she was having a panic attack."

"Right."

"Plus Ventura was a mob scene getting over here."

"OK."

"But how are *you*?" she asked.

"Man, I am great," he said. "So glad to be forty. You have no idea."

"When I turned forty, Chris O'Donnell flew me to the Bahamas," she said. "That did *not* go well."

"I can imagine," Brad said.

"In any case, I have good news for you."

"Is that right?"

"Yeah. After our meeting yesterday—which you fucked royally, I might add—Fox fired Trey Peters."

"Who?"

"The executive. The one who treated you like shit."

"Oh, right."

Brad noted to himself that he needed to try to remember things, even if he didn't. That was how it worked here anyway.

"Yeah, they didn't like his attitude at the meeting. Apparently, one of the other executives, the one who wasn't talking much, thought your idea was great."

"Really?"

"And they want to hear more on Monday."

"Wait," Brad said. "What was the idea again?"

Alison looked frustrated. "Do you want to succeed or not?"

"I do," Brad said. "Really, I do."

"It was about the infinite time loop. I had no idea what you were talking about. Did you?"

"I do now," Brad said.

"What does that mean?"

"It means I have a lot of material suddenly."

"Good," Alison said. "Don't blow it."

"I won't."

"Stay sober."

"I will stay *relatively* sober."

"I have more news for you too."

Alison went months without ever having *anything* for Brad. This really was a Golden Grahams day.

"What?" he said.

"They're rebooting *Battlecats*."

"Again?"

"I'm as surprised as you are. I always hated that show."

"Me too."

"Well, learn to like it. I got a call from the showrunner. They need people on staff who are familiar with the material."

Brad had seen enough *Battlecats* for twenty lifetimes. When you have a hundred childhoods, there are a lot of dead hours. Plus, in his most recent run-through, he'd actually worked on the show again.

"I'm supremely qualified," he said.

"It's an initial twelve-episode run," she said. "They'll pay you fifteen thousand dollars up front, plus some residual and back-end stuff that we'll negotiate."

"Wow," Brad said. "I'm actually going to be able to pay my rent for the rest of the year."

"If you sell that pilot, you'll be able to do more than that," she said.

Alison's phone made a noise. She looked down.

"Shit," she said.

"What?"

"My Pilates instructor got his hand caught in a blender."

"That sucks."

"He was making a smoothie."

"Right."

"And he needs me to drive him to the emergency room."

"Of course."

"So I'm going to go."

"Sure."

"This is the part where you thank me."

"Of course. Thank you. For everything. I will not blow this."

"You might," she said.

And then she walked out.

Alison was right, of course. Brad might blow this. He might blow everything. There was no guarantee anything would go well or that he would make all the right decisions. Circumstances rarely tilted in anyone's favor. Why would they necessarily tilt in his?

On his way home he stopped at a florist to buy something nice for Juliet and the girls. They'd been without him for a very long time, whether they knew it or not. Flowers were just the beginning. He also stopped at a different store and bought something floral for himself. Living four thousand years had taught him a lot of lessons, but giving up marijuana wasn't one of them.

But from now on, being a stoner wouldn't be his *primary* commitment. Brad would be there for his family. Not that he'd been absent or neglectful before, but now he would really be *with them*, in the moment, whatever they needed, whenever they needed. It would be his duty, his obligation, and his pleasure.

His youth was over now for good. There were plenty of decent years left, but the body would shortly begin its wind down. At a certain point the announcers in the erectile-dysfunction ads would be speaking directly to him. He would experience the middle-aged hassles of achy knees and bum hips. There would also still be afternoons spent waiting on hold with Time Warner so that he could yell at someone in person. He was going to have car trouble. Some dude in a big blue pickup would cut him off in traffic. At some point someone would serve him a sandwich with mayo on it, even though he'd *specifically* told them not to. People would be greedy and selfish and rude and cruel. There would be so much Twitter and Facebook and Instagram and Foursquare and Tumblr and Pinterest and LinkedIn and Snapchat and all the social media bullshit that was getting ready to wash over the culture. He had no real way to avoid hearing about Justin Bieber or about Mitt Romney's presidential campaign. Also, the global climactic apocalypse was coming. No one was going to stop it, and everyone was going to suffer. Even worse, and he didn't know it, the Giants were about to win two of the next three World Series. That would be the ultimate indignity.

But Brad wanted something new so badly that he would take all of that in excellent stride, other than the Giants winning—the only thing that would leave him begging for a return to his infinite time loop. But other than that ultimate disaster, he was finally, mercifully, going to get to see 2011, 2012, *2013*, and onward. The future would be a mystery to him. Whatever happened, he was ready to watch it unfold.

His career might blossom or he might flop yet again. Maybe he'd live in his crappy house forever, or maybe he'd end up in a nice house full of nice-house problems. Either way, his wife would witch on, and his daughters would blossom. He'd go to Florida and see his parents again, appreciate the hundred times they'd raised him, and find them annoying as always. They were going to get sick. They were going to get old. They were going to die. So was he. It would all end badly, in poverty, madness, incontinence, and desperate pain, like it does for almost everyone. Brad welcomed it all. He was desperate to experience life's back nine.

He pulled up to the house. Juliet was waiting for him.

"How's it going?" she said.

"Good!" he said. "I got a gig. They're remaking *Battlecats*."

"Again?"

"I said the same thing. But it's a paycheck. Plus I have a pitch meeting on Monday."

"For what?"

"That infinite time loop thing," he said.

"You and your infinite time loops," said Juliet.

"It's a potent formula," Brad said.

"Speaking of potent formulas, I just sold a thousand bucks' worth of potions to this Wiccan group in Iowa City."

"That's unexpected."

"Not really," Juliet said. "I'm good."

"Sometimes you're *too* good," he said.

"What do you mean?"

"After what you did to me."

"And what did I do to you?" she said.

"Gave me that potion."

"Did you sleep?" she asked.

"Yes."

"Do you feel better?"

"Yes."

"Then that's what I did to you."

Brad took Juliet in his arms and kissed her—hard but not too hard. He'd learned she didn't respond well to desperation.

"Why the passion?" she said.

"It's been too long," he said.

Brad and Juliet lived in the crappiest rental house in Southern California. Their careers were unstable, their daughters understimulated, their health mediocre. The browning hills above them were nature's tinderbox. Humanity was probably going to end sometime in the next fifty to a hundred years. But for now they were flush, they were together, and they were happy. Brad Cohen enjoyed this moment like he'd never enjoyed another moment before in his life. Or any of his lives.

He couldn't wait for tomorrow.

ACKNOWLEDGMENTS

Thanks to the fine people at Amazon Publishing, including, but not limited to, Alan Turkus, Alex Carr, Brian Mitchell, Caroline Carr, Courtney Miller, Jeff Belle, Jodi Warshaw, Kristi Coulter, Terry Goodman, and Tiffany Pokorny. Thanks also to David Downing for giving this here book such a thoughtful read, my agent Daniel Greenberg, and fellow travelers Jami Attenberg, Deborah Reed, Owen Egerton, and Emily Gould for their friendship and support. Let's not forget my fellow *Jeopardy!* contestants, including, but not limited to, Hillary Kwiatek, Loni Geerlings, Jared Hall, and especially Sarah Zucker, the only person who's ever beaten me. Many thanks to the staff of *Jeopardy!*, particularly the contestant coordinators, for helping make my game-show dreams come true. And, as always, love and gratitude to my wife, Regina, and my son, Elijah, to whom I dedicate this book, in this life and all the lives to come.

ABOUT THE AUTHOR

Neal Pollack is an American satirist, novelist, short story writer, and journalist. Pollack has written eight books: *The Neal Pollack Anthology of American Literature*, *Never Mind the Pollacks*, *Beneath the Axis of Evil*, *Alternadad*, *Stretch*, *Jewball*, *Downward-Facing Death*, and *Open Your Heart*. A certified yoga instructor, international motorsports correspondent, and three-time *Jeopardy!* champion, Pollack lives in Austin, Texas, with his wife and son.